Dylan had the good sens... ...sorry. I didn't see you standing there. Did you sleep well?"

The expression of every woman within earshot was the same. Shock. Dismay. Vested calculation.

Mia wanted to tell them not to worry, but it didn't seem the time. She held out her arms for the baby. "I'll take her. Thanks for dinner. I'm surprised to see you looking so comfortable and domesticated with a baby. Or was that nothing but an act for your groupies?"

His eyebrows rose to his hairline, but still he didn't surrender the baby. "The little Mia I knew was never sarcastic."

"The little Mia you knew wouldn't say boo to a goose. I'm not a child anymore."

He stared at her. Hard. The way a man stares at a woman. "No, you definitely are not."

* * *

Baby for Keeps is part of the #1 bestselling miniseries from Harlequin Desire—Billionaires and Babies: Powerful men...wrapped around their babies' little fingers.

* * *

If you're on Twitter,
tell us what you think of Harlequin Desire!
#harlequindesire

Dear Reader,

Teaching elementary grades, as I did, can break your heart. In public school, classrooms are full of precious boys and girls whose home lives are difficult, unhappy or painful. How can children concentrate on learning adverbs when they worry about what's going on at home...or when they haven't slept for more than a few hours the night before?

Even kids from privileged backgrounds can struggle with the written word. School is not always a fun place when you don't learn in traditional ways. My hero had every opportunity in life, but still he stumbled.

Dylan and Mia are an unlikely couple on the surface. But as you well know, love finds its way in through the smallest of cracks. Throw a baby into the mix and the results are unpredictable and wonderful.

Wishing you a summer filled with laughter, simplicity, outdoor fun and long days of playing with family.

God bless,

Janice Maynard

BABY
FOR KEEPS

—

JANICE MAYNARD

Recycling programs
for this product may
not exist in your area.

ISBN-13: 978-0-373-73320-0

BABY FOR KEEPS

Copyright © 2014 by Janice Maynard

Printed in U.S.A.

www.Harlequin.com

JANICE MAYNARD

is a *USA TODAY* bestselling author who lives in beautiful east Tennessee with her husband. She holds a B.A. from Emory and Henry College and an M.A. from East Tennessee State University. In 2002 Janice left a fifteen-year career as an elementary school teacher to pursue writing full-time. Now her first love is creating sexy, character-driven, contemporary romance stories.

Janice loves to travel and enjoys using those experiences as settings for books. Hearing from readers is one of the best perks of the job! Visit her website, www.janicemaynard.com, and follow her on Facebook and Twitter.

I dedicate this book to children everywhere who think they are not smart. Don't ever believe it! It's a great big world out there. Follow your dreams...always!

One

Saturday nights were always busy at the Silver Dollar Saloon. Dylan Kavanagh surveyed the crowd with a gaze that catalogued every detail. The newlyweds at table six. The habitual drunk who would soon have to be booted out. The kid who looked nervous enough to be contemplating the use of a fake ID.

Around the bar—a winding expanse of wood that dated back to the 1800s and had been rescued from a building in Colorado—the usual suspects ordered drinks and munched on peanuts. The tourists were easy to spot, not only because Dylan knew most of the locals, but because the out-of-towners scanned the room eagerly, hoping to spot celebrities.

Western North Carolina's natural beauty drew people for many reasons. Families on vacation, for sure. But the state was also a hot spot for location scouts. Dylan's home, the elegant town of Silver Glen, was no stranger to famous faces. Just last week one of Hollywood's iconic directors had wrapped production on a civil-war picture.

Dylan shrugged inwardly. He had no interest at all in the famous or the infamous when it came to the world of filmmaking, no matter how many A-listers dropped by for a drink or a meal. Once burned, twice shy.

Suddenly, he realized that he had unconsciously been watching something that sent up a red flag. The woman at the other end of the bar was knocking back drinks at an alarming rate. He frowned, surprised that his head bartender, Rick, hadn't already cut her off.

Working his way behind the bar, Dylan inched closer to Rick. Two other servers were helping out because things were so hectic. And that wasn't counting the three waitresses handling food orders out on the floor.

When Dylan was in earshot of his employee, he tapped him on the shoulder and muttered, "You need to pull the plug on the lady in pink. She's had enough, I think." The woman exhibited an air of desperation that didn't mix well with alcohol.

Rick grinned, his big hands busy filling drink orders. "Not to worry, Boss. She's drinking virgin strawberry daiquiris."

"Ah." It was blisteringly hot outside, an airless summer evening that justified anyone having a cold one…or two or three. The AC was working very well in here right now, yet the woman swallowed her icy drinks with reckless precision. With a nod, Dylan moved away, aware that he was creating a traffic jam in the narrow space.

Rick, who was two decades his senior, cocked his head toward the door. "Go home, Boss. We got this." The big, burly man with the country accent was perfectly suited to his job. And he was a pro. He and the rest of the staff didn't need Dylan hovering and giving the impression he didn't trust them.

But the truth was, Dylan loved the Silver Dollar. He'd bought it as a twenty-year-old kid, and after renovating the old building from the ground up, he'd opened what was to become one of Silver Glen's most thriving businesses.

Dylan had been a wealthy man when he bought the bar. And if the place ever went belly-up, he'd be a rich man still. As one of the Kavanaghs, the family that put Silver Glen on the map back in the mid-twentieth century, Dylan could easily afford to spend his days and his dollars on idle living. But his mother, Maeve, had brought up all seven of her boys to respect the value of a hard day's work.

That wasn't why Dylan was hanging around the Silver Dollar on a Saturday night. He had put in plenty of hours this week. The reason was far more complex. This bar was proof—hard-core evidence—that he wasn't a total failure in life. Despite his youthful stumbles, he had made something of himself.

He didn't like thinking about his adolescence. Parts of it had been a nightmare. And the ugly reality that he was never going to match his older brother in academic achievement had tormented him right up until the day he admitted defeat and dropped out of college.

The truth was, he felt more like himself here at the saloon than most any other place. The Silver Dollar was laid-back, sometimes rowdy, and always interesting. It felt comfortable. Nobody here knew about his failings. No one, even the locals, seemed to remember that Dylan had been metaphorically voted "student most likely to be a bum."

He'd absolutely hated not being able to master the required subjects in school, but he had masked his anger and frustration by building a reputation for insolence, irresponsibility and wild partying.

Only when he had found this old building disintegrating and in disrepair had he finally settled down and found his passion. Like the building, there was more to Dylan than met the eye. But he'd had to prove himself. So the Silver Dollar was more than a project. It was his personal declaration of independence.

Besides, Dylan was *between relationships* at the moment, and he'd rather be here mingling than sitting at home watching summer reruns. He was a people person, plain and simple. That brought him back to the puzzle of the woman in pink.

Ignore her. Rick was right. Dylan *should* go home. As much as he enjoyed spending time at the Silver Dollar, there was more to life than business. Before he departed, though, he knew he had to check on his unusual and intriguing customer. When the stool beside her became available, Dylan took it as a sign. He had Irish blood running in his veins. Sometimes the universe pointed toward a clear and obvious path.

It wasn't strange to have a single lady drinking at the bar. But the ones who did were usually trolling for a pickup. This slight, harried-looking woman seemed to be encased in a bubble of solitude, her eyes focused on her drink. Quietly, he sat down to her left and only then saw what he hadn't been able to see from his previous vantage point.

She was holding a baby.

An infant, to be exact. Cradled in the woman's right arm, resting in her lap, was a tiny, sleeping child. A girl, if the little pink ribbon stuck to her one curl of dark hair was any indication.

Already regretting his impulse, Dylan assessed the situation instantly, realizing that more was at work here than a woman needing a drink. If he were smart, he would back away. His impulse to wade in and help people often went unappreciated, or even worse, blew up in his face.

When the woman didn't so much as acknowledge his presence, even though they were sitting practically hip to hip, his gut told him to stand up and walk away. He would have. He should have. But just then the slender female plopped her glass on the bar, hiccupped and gave one of those little multiple-hitching sighs that said louder than words she had been crying, was about to cry or was trying *not* to cry.

Female tears scared the crap out of Dylan. He was no different than any other member of his sex in that regard.

He had grown up without sisters, and the last time he saw his mother cry was at his dad's funeral years ago. So the urge to run made complete sense.

But something held him in his seat. Some gut-deep, chivalrous desire to help. That, and the faint female scent that made him think of summer roses blooming in the gardens up at the Silver Beeches, his brother's ritzy hotel on top of the mountain.

Still debating what he should say or do, he paused for another careful, sideways glance. His mystery lady was sitting down, so it was hard to gauge her height, but *average* was his best guess. She wore khaki pants and a pale pink, button-down shirt. Dark brown hair pulled back in a ragged ponytail revealed her delicate profile and a pointed chin with a bit of a stubborn tilt.

Something about her was very familiar, perhaps because she reminded him of the actress Zooey Deschanel, only without the smile or the joie de vivre. The woman at Dylan's side was the picture of exhaustion. Her left hand no longer held a drink, but even at rest, it fisted on the bar. No wedding ring. That, however, could mean anything.

Stand up. Walk away.

His subconscious tried to help him, it really did. But sometimes a man had to do what a man had to do. Grimacing inwardly, he leaned a bit closer to be heard over the music and the high-decibel conversations surrounding them. "Excuse me, ma'am. I'm Dylan Kavanagh, the owner here. Are you okay? Is there anything I can do to help?"

If Mia hadn't been holding her daughter, Cora, so tightly, she might have dropped the sleeping baby. The shock of hearing Dylan's voice after so many years burned through her stupor of despair and fatigue and ripped at her nerve endings. She had walked into the Silver Dollar because she heard he was the owner and because she was curious about how things had turned out for him. She hadn't really expected him to be here.

Looking up, she bit her lip. "Hello, Dylan. It's me. Mia. Mia Larin."

The poleaxed look that crossed his face wasn't flattering. Only a blind woman could have missed the mix of emotions that was a long way from "Great to see you." He recovered quickly, though. "Good Lord. Mia Larin. What brings you back to Silver Glen?"

It was a reasonable question. She hadn't lived here since the year she and Dylan graduated from high school. He had been eighteen and full of piss and vinegar. She had been sixteen and scared of what lay ahead. She'd also been a social misfit with an IQ near 170 and little else to commend her. While she was in graduate school, her parents had sold the family home and retired to the Gulf Coast, thus severing her last connection to Silver Glen.

She shrugged, feeling her throat close up at the memories. "I don't really know. Nostalgia, I guess. How are you doing?"

It was a stupid question. She could *see* how he was doing. The boy with the skinny, rangy frame had filled out, matured, taken a second helping of tall, dark and gorgeous. His warm, whiskey-brown eyes locked on hers and made her stomach do a free fall, even though she was sitting down.

Broad shoulders and a headful of thick, golden-chestnut hair, along with a hard, muscled body added up to a man who oozed masculinity. She wondered if he was still as much of a badass as he had been as a teenager. Back then his aim in life seemed to be seeking out trouble.

He was the first boy she'd ever had as a friend, the only boy who had ever kissed her, until she got out of college.

And here he was, looking too damned appealing for his own good.

Dylan grinned, the flash of his smile a blow to her already damaged heart. In an instant, she was back in school, heartsick with a desperate crush that was laced with the knowledge she had as much chance of ever becoming Dylan Kavanagh's girlfriend as she did of being voted Homecoming Queen.

He raised a hand, and at some unseen signal, the bartender brought him a club soda with lime. Dylan took a drink, set down his glass and flicked the end of her ponytail. "You've grown up."

The three laconic words held equal measures of surprise and male interest. Her stupid heart responded with adolescent pleasure despite the fact that she was now past thirty, held two doctoral degrees and, as of twelve weeks ago, had become a mother.

"So have you." Though it galled her to admit it, she couldn't hold his gaze. She was no longer the painfully shy girl she had been when he knew her before, but even the most confident of women would have to admit that Dylan Kavanagh was a bit overwhelming at close range.

He toyed with the straw in his glass, not bothering to disguise his curiosity as he looked down at Cora. The baby, bless her heart, was sleeping blissfully. It was only at two in the morning that she usually showed any aversion to slumber.

"So you have a child," he said.

"What tipped you off, smart guy?"

He winced.

Appalled, she realized that her careless comment must have sounded like a reference to the past. She'd tutored him because he had dyslexia. As a senior, Dylan had hated being forced to take help from a classmate, especially one who had skipped two grades and was only fifteen. The pride of a cocky teenage boy had taken a beating at having Mia witness his inability to read and master English textbooks and novels.

"That's not what I meant," she said quickly. "I'm sorry. I'm a little self-conscious about having a baby and not being married. My parents are adjusting, but they don't like it."

"So where's the kid's dad?" Dylan seemed to have forgiven Mia for her awkward comment. His eyes registered more than a passing interest in the answer to his question as he waited.

"I'm not really prepared to go into that."

The man on her right reared back in raucous laughter and jostled her roughly. Mia cuddled Cora more tightly, realizing that a bar was the last place in the world she should have brought her infant daughter.

Dylan must have come to the same conclusion, because he put a hand on her arm and smiled persuasively. "We can't talk here. Let's go upstairs and get comfortable. It used to be my bookkeeper's apartment, but she moved out last Tuesday."

Mia allowed him to help her to her feet. Grabbing the diaper bag she'd propped on the foot rail, she slung it over her shoulder. "That would be nice." For a woman with a genius IQ, she probably should have been able to come up with a better adjective. But this encounter seemed surreal. Her social skills were rusty at best. Given the fact that she hadn't slept a full night since Cora had been born, it was no wonder *nice* was the best she could do..

"Follow me." Dylan led her across the restaurant floor to a hallway at the back of the building. The steep, narrow staircase at the end was dimly lit.

He insisted on taking the diaper bag and would have taken Cora as well, but Mia clutched her tightly. "I can carry her." She trailed in his wake as they ascended, trying not to ogle his tight butt packaged nicely in well-washed jeans.

She knew the man in front of her was a millionaire several times over. Yet somehow, he had the knack of appearing to be just one of the guys. It was a talent she had envied in high school. Mia hadn't fit in with any crowd or clique. Shy and serious, she had been all but ostracized by her classmates who were two years or more ahead of her in adolescence.

On the landing, Dylan paused, giving her a chance to catch up. "The area to our left is storage. As I said, this apartment up here was my bookkeeper's. But she got engaged and moved across the country. You can imagine what a mess I've made of things. I need to hire somebody soon or I'll have the IRS on my back for not paying my quarterly taxes."

He opened the nearest door and ushered her inside. Mia looked around with interest. They stood in a good-size living area furnished with a sofa, loveseat and two chairs upholstered in a navy-and-taupe print. The neutral rug was clean but unexceptional. Faded patches on the walls indicated where pictures had hung. "How long was she with you?"

Dylan dropped the diaper bag on a chair. "Nearly since the beginning. Her first husband died and left her with almost nothing. So this job was a godsend both for her and for me. But a couple of months ago, she met a trucker downstairs, and the rest is history."

Mia sank onto the sofa with a sigh and laid Cora beside her. The baby didn't stir. "Life is full of surprises."

He sprawled in a chair at her elbow. "It sure as hell is. You remember my brother Liam?"

"Of course I do. He always scared me a little bit. So serious and intimidating."

"He's loosened up a lot since he met Zoe. She's his new

wife. You should meet her. The two of you would probably get along."

"Really? Why?"

Obviously his throwaway statement was meant to be rhetorical, because he hesitated. "Oh, you know. Girl stuff…"

Her face flushed. This was always her problem. She had never mastered the art of careless chitchat. Fussing with Cora's blanket for a moment gave her a chance to look away. She should probably go. But she'd made such a complete and total mess of her life, she was deeply grateful to have an excuse to focus on someone other than herself for a moment. Gathering her composure, she leaned back and gave Dylan a pleasant smile. "Well, other than your brother's marriage, what's been going on in Silver Glen since I've been gone?"

Dylan propped an ankle on the other knee and tucked his hands behind his head. "Have you had dinner?" It wasn't an answer to Mia's question, but he was starving.

"No. Not really. But you don't have to feed me."

"It's on the house. For old time's sake." He pulled out his cell phone and sent a text to the kitchen. "They'll bring something up as soon as they can."

"Sounds good." Mia's smile was shy. He remembered the slight duck of her head and the curve of soft pink lips when something pleased her. Not that pleasing Mia had been Dylan's forte. He'd resented like hell the fact that he had to take help from a fifteen-year-old kid. And truth be told, he had probably made Mia's life a misery more often than not.

"Why did you do it?" he asked. The question tumbled out. He hadn't even known he was going to ask it.

A slight frown creased her forehead. "Do what?"

"Tutor me." His face was somber.

"Wow, Dylan. It's taken you this long to ask that question?"

He shrugged, making her more aware than ever of the breadth of his shoulders. "I was busy before."

"You were, at that," she agreed. "Football, basketball, dating hot girls."

"You noticed?"

"I noticed everything," she said flatly. "I had the worst crush on you."

He blanched, remembering all his careless cruelties to her. Even though in private he'd been pathetically grateful when she helped him make sense of a Shakespeare play, in public he had shunned her...or made jokes about her. Even at the time, with all the cluelessness of an adolescent boy, he'd known he was hurting her.

But maintaining his image as a badass had been his one and only goal. While some of his classmates were getting scholarship offers from Duke or the University of North Carolina, Dylan had struggled to pretend he didn't care. College was stupid and unnecessary. He'd said it enough times that he almost believed it. But when he slunk off to community college and couldn't even make passing grades there, his humiliation was complete.

"I owe you about a million apologies," he said, his mouth twisting in a grimace of regret. "You tried so hard to help me."

"I might point out that you did pass senior English."

"True. And without cheating, if you remember."

"You wrote an essay about why Romeo and Juliet was such an unbelievable story."

"Well, it was," he protested. "What kind of idiot takes poison when he could have kidnapped the girl and run away to Vegas?"

Mia chuckled, the laughter erasing her air of exhaustion and making her look more like the girl he'd known in high school. "It wasn't your fault, Dylan. The problems you had. Someone should have diagnosed you in elementary school, and your educational career would have been entirely different."

"You can't blame them too much. I did a damned good job of pretending that I was lazy and unmotivated."

"You may have fooled a lot of people, but you never fooled me."

Two

Dylan's wry smile and self-deprecating assessment made Mia's heart hurt. Dyslexia was no minor roadblock. Mia knew that Dylan had scored above average on intelligence tests. When it came to creating ideas and working with people, he far outstripped her in ability. Dylan was smart and gifted. Unfortunately, his talents didn't align with the way traditional education evaluated achievement.

She circled back to his earlier question. "You asked me why I tutored you."

"Well, why did you?"

"I suppose it was for lots of reasons. For one thing, the teacher asked me to. And for another, I was no different than any other girl at Silver Glen High. I wanted to spend time with you."

He rubbed his jaw. "Is that all?"

"No." Time for brutal honesty. "I wanted you to succeed. And I thought I could help. No matter how hard you tried to pretend differently, I knew you hated feeling—"

"Stupid," he interjected with some heat. "The word you're looking for is *stupid*."

She stared at him, taken aback that his intelligence still seemed to be a sore spot for him. "Good grief, Dylan. You're a successful, respected businessman. You work for a living even though you don't have to. You've made the Silver Dollar Saloon into something special. Why does it matter *now* that you struggled in school? We're not kids anymore. You've more than proven your capabilities."

His jaw clenched, his eyes stormy, though somehow she knew his agitation was not directed at her. "And what about you, Mia? What do you do?"

"I'm a medical researcher. Over in the Raleigh/Durham area. My team has been working to prove that the standard series of childhood vaccines is safe for everyone."

"And I sell beer for a living."

"Don't be flip," she said, her temper starting to rise. "It's not a competition."

"Of course not. I was never competition for you. How many languages do you speak?"

His sarcasm nicked her in ways she couldn't explain. She hadn't asked to be smart. In fact, there had been many days in her life when she would have given almost anything to be the epitome of a dumb blonde joke. She glanced at Cora, who was still sleeping peacefully.

"I should go," she said quietly. "I didn't mean to stir up the past. It was nice seeing you again." A chill of disappointment clenched her heart and brought back unpleasant memories of being out of step with the world.

She and Dylan stood at the same moment.

His face registered consternation and shame. "Don't leave. I'm being an ass. It's not your fault you're a genius."

"I'm a woman," she said flatly. "And will it make you feel better to know that I've made an absolute mess of my life?" Her voice broke on the last word. Tears she had worked so hard to keep at bay for the past several hours burst forth in an unattractive sobbing mess.

Inside her chest, a great gaping hole filled with uncertainty and fear made it hard to breathe. She didn't feel smart at all. What she really felt was panicked and desperate.

She put her hands over her face, mortified that Dylan was here to witness her inevitable meltdown.

Without warning, she felt his warm hands on her shoulders. "Sit down, Mia. Everything's going to be all right."

"You don't know that," she said, sniffling and, as usual, without a tissue.

"Here. Take this." The pristine square of white cotton he pulled from his back pocket was still warm from his body. She blew her nose and wiped her eyes, feeling hollow and shaky.

Dylan tugged her down beside him on the sofa, both of them glancing at Cora automatically to make sure she was in no danger. The baby was oblivious. "Don't worry," she said, trying to laugh. "I'm not going to have a nervous breakdown."

He grinned, revealing the slightest hint of a dimple. "Why don't you tell me what's going on?"

"It's a long story."

"I've got all night."

The genuine concern in his eyes disarmed her, despite her embarrassment. It couldn't hurt to have an impartial opinion. She was at a crossroads, and perhaps she was too close to the situation and too sleep-deprived to make a rational decision.

"Okay," she said. "You asked for it."

"Start at the beginning." He stretched a muscular arm along the back of the sofa, making her uncomfortably aware of his masculine scent and closeness. His khaki slacks and navy knit polo shirt with the bar's name embroidered on the chest fit him in a way that emphasized everything about him that was male.

Her hands shook, so she clasped them in her lap. "After I turned twenty-nine, I realized that I wanted a baby. A cliché, I know, but my biological clock was ticking so loudly, I couldn't ignore it."

"Did the man in your life agree?"

"There was no man at that moment. Well, there was one. For about fifteen minutes. But we were a terrible match, and thankfully we both recognized it before we did anything irrevocable."

"So who did you have in mind for a daddy?"

"Nobody," she said simply. "I was well educated and financially secure. I decided that I could raise a child on my own." She couldn't fault the skepticism she saw on his face. In retrospect, she had been both naive and overly confident in her abilities.

"There's still the matter of sperm."

His droll comment made her cheeks heat again. "Well, of course, but I had that all figured out. As part of the scientific community in Raleigh, I possessed a working knowledge of what was going on in most of our experimental labs. And of course, fertility research was and still is a majorly funded arm of study."

"Still no sperm."

"I'm getting there. Once I found a doctor and a facility that I trusted, I had all the initial tests to see if I was healthy and ovulating well."

"And were you?"

"Definitely. So I knew the timing was right. Then all I had to do was visit a sperm bank and select the proper donor."

"Who, I'm assuming, would be a doctoral student with intellectual capabilities matching your own."

He was entirely serious.

She shook her head vehemently. "No. Not even close. I would never do that to a child of mine. I wanted a normal baby."

"Good Lord, Mia. You mean to tell me you deliberately tried to make little Cora less smart than her mother?" The baffled shock on his face gave her a moment's pause.

"I wouldn't say that." She heard the defensiveness in her words and winced inwardly. "But I selected a candidate who was a blue-collar worker with average intelligence."

"Why?"

"I wanted her to have a happy life."

Dylan honestly didn't know what to say. *I wanted her to have a happy life.* Those eight words, quietly spoken, told him more about Mia than if he'd had her résumé in front of him. For the first time, he understood that even if his school career had been painful and difficult, Mia's had also, but in an entirely different way.

The knock on the door saved him from having to respond to that last, heart-wrenching statement. Soon he and Mia were enjoying appetizers and burgers. Based on the drinks she had ordered downstairs, he avoided anything alcoholic and instead opted for Cokes to accompany their meal.

Mia ate like she hadn't eaten in a week. "This food is amazing," she said. "Thank you so much. I've been living off frozen dinners and frozen pizza for days. My mom helped out for the first week and a half, but the baby exhausted her, so I finally encouraged her to go home."

He lifted an eyebrow, helping himself to another handful of French fries. "You've left me hanging," he said. "Finish your story, please."

"I was hoping you'd lost interest. The whole sorry tale doesn't put me in a very good light."

When she wiped a dab of ketchup from her lower lip, to his surprise, he felt a little zing that was a lot like sexual interest. Squashing that thought, he leaned back in his chair. "I'm all ears."

Mia was slender and graceful. Though she wore neither makeup nor jewelry, she carried herself with an inherent femininity. Back in high school, he had kissed her once upon a time, more out of curiosity than anything else. The heat had surprised and alarmed him. He needed Mia's help with schoolwork. He couldn't afford to alienate her, just because his teenage libido was revving on all cylinders.

Now, thinking back to how he had perceived the fifteen-year-old Mia, he wondered what had attracted him. She'd been quiet and timid, although she *had* managed to stand up to him on more than one occasion when he tried to blow off a project or an assignment.

Her looks and figure had been nothing spectacular in the eyes of a teenage boy. Mia had been on the cusp of womanhood, with no breasts to speak of, and a body that was still girlish despite her maturity in other ways. Yet something about her had appealed to him. In all of their interactions, she had never once made fun of his ineptitude, nor had she patronized him.

Now, from the vantage point of adulthood, he marveled that she had put up with his arrogance and antagonism. Though eventually they had become friends, for weeks at the beginning of their relationship he had acted like a total jerk. And an ungrateful jerk at that.

He kept silent, counting on the fact that she would eventually talk to him if he didn't push.

Mia finished the last swallow of her drink, stacked her dishes neatly and curled her legs beneath her. "The thing is," she said, wrinkling her nose as if about to confess to a crime, "artificial insemination is expensive. I assumed, quite erroneously, that since I was young and healthy I would get pregnant the first time."

"But you didn't."

"No. And every month when I got my period, I cried."

"Why was it so important to you?"

She blinked, her expression one of shock, as though no one had ever dared ask her that question. "I wanted someone of my own to love. You may not remember, but my folks were older parents. They had me when my mom was forty-three. So though I love them very much, I understood why they wanted to retire and move south. Even when we lived in the same state, we didn't see that much of each other."

"Why not?"

She hesitated. "They were proud because I was smart, but they had no idea what to do with me. Once I was out on my own, the gulf widened. I'm sure part of it was my fault. I never quite understood how to talk to them about my work. And besides…"

"Go on."

"I found out when I was a teenager that my parents had never really wanted children. It was a Pandora's box kind of thing. I read one of my mom's journals. Turns out that when I was conceived, my mother was going through menopause and thought she couldn't get pregnant. So I was an unwelcome surprise in more ways than one. They did the best they could. I'm grateful for that."

Dylan thought of his big, close-knit, sometimes rowdy family. And of the way his mother cherished and coddled each of her sons though they were now grown men. They all had their moments of discord, of course. What family didn't? But he couldn't imagine a life where his brothers and his mom weren't an integral part of who he was. "I'm sorry," he said quietly. "That must have hurt."

Mia shrugged. "Anyway, you asked why the baby was so important. The truth is, I wanted someone to love who would love me back. I wanted a family of my own." She laid a hand gently on the baby's blanket. "It took eight tries, but when the doctor told me I was pregnant, it was the most wonderful day of my life."

Since Dylan had witnessed her tears not so long ago, he surmised that the euphoria hadn't lasted. "Was the pregnancy difficult?"

"Oh, no. Not at all."

"And did people ask questions?"

"My staff was actually fairly small. And we each worked on a particular aspect of the project. So we were more like professional acquaintances than the kind of deeper connections you sometimes make in an office environment. My friend Janette knew the truth. Frankly, she thought it was a bad idea all along…tried to talk me out of it more than once. But she was supportive once I actually became pregnant. She even went with me to childbirth classes and stayed with me at the hospital when Cora was born."

"So what went wrong? Why did you come back to Silver Glen and walk into my bar?"

She leaned her head against the back of the sofa, her gaze bleak. "A dreadful domino of events. My job paid well, and I had a healthy savings portfolio. But I drained all of it trying to get pregnant. Even that didn't seem *so* irresponsible, because I knew that I could live on a strict budget and build up my savings again. Only I hadn't counted on the fickle finger of fate."

"Meaning?"

"While I was on maternity leave, the funding for my research and my lab was eliminated. Big-time budget cuts. So now I had a brand-new baby and no job. And, as a wonderful dollop of icing on the cake, my roommate with whom I rented a condo decided to move in with her boyfriend."

He leaned forward and rested his hands on his knees, smiling at her with an abundance of sympathy. "That sucks."

She managed a somewhat teary chuckle. "I probably wouldn't be such a basket case if little Cora here slept at night. But no matter how many books I read and how many theories I try, all she wants to do is snooze during the day and play all night."

"I don't blame her. That's my M.O. sometimes."

His droll humor made her smile, when the last thing she felt like doing was smiling. She remembered that about him. Dylan was always the life of the party. He could rally a crowd around a cause, and best of all, he wasn't moody. Some guys like him, i.e. rich and handsome, were egotists. But Dylan was the opposite.

He'd spent his high school years trying to prove that he was one of the gang. No one special.

She felt embarrassed suddenly. He must think she was a total nutcase. It was time to go. But just as she was gathering herself to depart, little Cora stirred and cried out.

Dylan's face softened as he focused on the tiny hands that flailed above the edge of the blanket. "Somebody is about to get mad."

"I need to feed her."

"Do you have baby food with you? I can send one of the staff to the store to get some."

"Um…no…thanks. *I* need to feed her. You know… nurse her."

His neck turned red. She could swear his gaze brushed across her breasts before landing somewhere on the far wall. "Of course. No problem. There's a comfy chair in the bedroom. Will that work?"

"That would be perfect." She rummaged in the bag for a clean diaper and a pack of baby wipes, conscious that he noted her every move. "I won't be too long. But don't feel like you have to entertain me. It's been fun catching up. I'll leave when I'm done."

He stood when she did, watching intently as she scooped Cora into her arms and bounced her so the baby's displeasure didn't escalate into a full-blown crying fit. Fortunately, Cora settled down and even smiled.

"Don't be ridiculous," Dylan said. "I don't want you to rush off. In fact, I'd love to hold Cora for a little while when you're done. Would you mind?"

She gaped at him. Big, brawny Dylan Kavanagh wanted to hold a baby? The thought sent a warm curl of *something* humming in the pit of her stomach. What was it about men and babies that made women go all gooey inside? "Of course I don't mind. But don't you have things to do?"

He tucked his hands in his back pockets and shook his head, his face alight with mischief. "Are you kidding? Mia Larin has come back to town all grown up. This is the most interesting encounter I've had in a month. Go feed the little one. I'll be here when you get back."

Three

Dylan watched Mia walk into the bedroom and push the door closed, though the latch didn't click shut. His brain whirled with a dozen thoughts and emotions as he wondered what would have happened if he hadn't sat down beside her at the bar. Would Mia have taken the baby back out to the car and driven away?

The thought made him uneasy. Had she sought him out on purpose, or was their meeting an accident?

He paced the room, wondering how long it took a woman to nurse a baby. Thinking about Mia baring her breasts and feeding her child was not wise. He had the weirdest urge to go in there and watch. Such a normal, *human* activity shouldn't affect him so strongly. Maybe it was because in his memories Mia was little more than a young girl herself.

Women were always at a disadvantage when it came to child rearing. It was all well and good to say a mother could have everything—career and family life. But it required a hell of a lot of juggling and tag-team parenting to make it work. Dylan's mother, when widowed long ago with seven boys, had leaned on her eldest son, Liam, to help carry the load.

Mia had no one.

Dylan could have gone back downstairs for a few minutes. He could have turned on the television. He could have sat down and relaxed after a long day. But instead, he paced. Things he didn't even know he remembered came rushing back from his subconscious. The way young Mia had chewed on the ends of her erasers. The little huffing sound of exasperation she made when she thought Dylan wasn't trying hard enough. The small frown that appeared between her eyebrows when she concentrated.

Oddly enough, he had found the eraser thing endearing. It made her seem human. Most of the time Mia's grasp of the kind of books that befuddled Dylan either baffled him or angered him or embarrassed him. As an adult, he understood that his academic difficulties were the result of a very specific problem. But he still reacted to the memories with an inward wince that told him he had a chip on his shoulder, even now.

Without thinking about what he was doing, he worked his way toward the bedroom door. Because the door didn't latch and because it was old and not level, the crack between the door and the frame had gradually widened. Dylan stood mesmerized, seeing only a slice of the room beyond. But it was enough to witness the quiet radiance on Mia's face. The way she looked at her baby made his chest tighten.

He rested a hand on the doorframe, swallowing hard as he realized that one of Mia's breasts was bare. He couldn't really see all that much from his vantage point. Spying on her was unforgiveable. But he couldn't look away from the picture of mother and child. The entire world was made up of moments like these, day after day.

For Dylan, however, it was brand-new. Witnessing it wrenched something inside his chest. Seeing Liam with Zoe these past few months had made Dylan vulnerable somehow…as if he couldn't help but wonder whether he would ever want that kind of tie…that kind of bond.

As Mia buttoned her blouse, he retreated hurriedly. By

the time she walked into the living room, he was leafing through a magazine that had been left behind. He looked up and smiled. "Is her tummy full?"

"It is indeed. She's very happy at the moment if you were serious about holding her."

"Of course I was." As he took the baby from Mia, his hand brushed her chest inadvertently. He was a grown man. It shouldn't have embarrassed him. But all he could think about was the curve of Mia's breast as she offered it to this infant. He turned away so he could hide the fact that he was flustered. "She's beautiful."

"I think so, but I suppose I'm prejudiced."

In his peripheral vision he saw Mia sit down on the sofa again. He circled the room slowly, singing nonsense songs, crooning bits of nursery rhymes he remembered from his childhood. He could swear that Cora's big, dark eyes, so like her mother's, focused on his face.

Half turning, he spoke softly. "She's going to be a charmer. I think she's flirting with me." When there was no response from Mia, he looked over his shoulder. She was curled up on the sofa, her cheek pillowed on one hand. Apparently she had plopped down and simply gone to sleep. Instantly.

He shook his head at Cora. "You're going to have to give Mommy a break, little one. She's worn out."

Debating his options, he decided to sneak downstairs and let Mia rest. The town had declared all public buildings no-smoking zones last year, so there would be nothing to harm the baby. And besides, Mia had been the one to bring her child into the bar. Surely she wouldn't mind.

Mia awoke slowly, completely disoriented. Had Cora cried out? She listened for a moment, and then in a blinding rush of recollection she realized where she was. But as she sat up and glanced around, she noted that her daughter and Dylan were nowhere to be found.

Telling herself there was no need to panic, she scrubbed her hands over her face and tried to shake off the feeling of being drugged. The nap had helped, but it wasn't the same as a full night's sleep. She stood up and stretched.

Grabbing her things, she smoothed her shirt and her hair and walked downstairs. The bar was still noisy and busy. When she actually looked at her watch, she groaned. It was after midnight. She found Dylan seated in a booth playing patty-cake with her baby. Standing two deep at his elbow was a group of fawning women. Now *this* was the Dylan she remembered. She wasn't sure, however, that she appreciated his using her baby as entertainment for his admirers.

Behind the bar, the big man who had poured her drinks earlier sketched a wave as he continued serving customers. Good heavens, what must Dylan's employees think of Mia's presence? Of Cora's?

Screwing up her courage, she edged toward the booth. Though she was no longer a social disaster, approaching a cluster of strangers still wasn't easy for her. She cleared her throat to attract Dylan's attention. "I need to go," she said.

Dylan had the good sense to look abashed. "Sorry. I didn't see you standing there. Did you sleep well?"

The expression of every woman in earshot was the same. Shock. Dismay. Vested calculation.

Mia wanted to tell them not to worry, but it didn't seem the time. She held out her arms for Cora. "I'll take her. Thanks for dinner."

As Dylan wiggled his way out of the booth, his entourage melted away. He moved closer to Mia, forcing the two of them into an intimate circle. "Don't be in such a damned hurry."

She put her hands over Cora's ears, scowling. "Watch

your mouth. I'm surprised to see you looking so comfortable and domesticated with Cora. Or was that nothing but an act for your groupies?"

His eyebrows rose to his hairline, but still he didn't surrender the baby. "The little Mia I knew was never sarcastic."

"The little Mia you knew wouldn't say *boo* to a goose. I'm not a child anymore."

He stared at her. Hard. The way a man stares at a woman. "No, you definitely are not."

It appeared that the man flirted indiscriminately, because she knew for a fact that he had no interest in her. "Give me my child."

Holding Cora even more tightly, he nodded his head toward the back. "I've got a closet-size office back there. Give me fifteen minutes. Then if you want to go, I won't stop you."

She was confused and tired and more than a little depressed. But short of wrestling him to the ground and making a scene, it appeared she had no choice. "Fine. Fifteen minutes."

Dylan's office was a wreck. He must have been telling the truth about his bookkeeper, because there was easily a week's worth of receipts and purchase orders stacked haphazardly across the surface of the scarred oak table he used as a desk. Still holding Cora, he motioned Mia into one of two chairs in the small space. "I have a proposition for you."

"You must be hard up if you're propositioning a nursing mom with a bad haircut and legs that haven't been shaved in two weeks."

This time she definitely saw him wince. "You used to be a lot sweeter, Mia Larin."

"I'm a mom now. I can't be a pushover. Are you ever going to give her back to me?"

He kissed the top of Cora's downy head. "You forget that I have five brothers younger than me. I've changed more than my share of diapers over the years."

"But not recently."

"No. Not recently."

If he had an agenda for this awkward meeting, he was taking his good easy time getting to the point. "What do you want from me, Dylan?"

His smile could have charmed the bloomers off an old-maid schoolteacher. "I want to offer you a job."

"Doing what?"

He waved a hand at the mess. "Being my new bookkeeper."

"That's absurd. I'm not an accountant."

He propped a hip against the table, forcing her to look at all the places his jeans were soft and worn. "You're a genius," he said, the words oddly inflected. "Keeping the books for the Silver Dollar Saloon isn't exactly rocket science."

"I don't need you to bail me out, Dylan. But thanks for the offer." Watching him absently stroke her daughter's hair undermined her hurry to leave. Dylan was big and strong and unabashedly masculine. But his hands held Cora gently.

"We'd be helping each other," he insisted. "The job comes with room and board. Or at least until you get tired of the food downstairs. I live five miles away, so you don't have to worry about me getting underfoot. There's an alarm system. You would be perfectly safe alone here when we're closed. I know the bar gets pretty noisy at times, but a fan or a sound machine would probably do the trick. The insulation between the floors is actually pretty good."

"Why are you doing this?"

"You need some time to regroup. I need a bookkeeper.

You won't have to worry about day care. Cora is welcome here always. And with a salary coming in—though I'm sure it's not even in the ballpark of what you were making in your field— you'll be comfortable and settled while you look for a new position."

It was a testament to her desperation that she considered it. Her résumé would have to be updated before she could job hunt. And the thought of spending more time with Cora was irresistible. Doing Dylan's books could be handled while Cora napped. But still she wasn't satisfied.

Shaking her head, she studied his face. "You can't tell me that you offer jobs to every hard-luck case who walks through the door. Why me? Why now?"

"I think you know why," he said quietly, meeting her gaze squarely. "I owe you more than I can ever repay. I'm sorry that I was a stupid teenage boy too proud to acknowledge what you were doing for me. But I'm saying it now. Thank you, Mia. For everything. The job is real. Please let me do this for you. It would mean a lot to me."

"You're serious? It was a long time ago, Dylan. And I liked tutoring you. You don't owe me anything."

"Then do it for Cora. Before you lost your job, you would have had to go back to work soon. Now you have a chance to spend several more weeks with her. Isn't that enough to make you say yes?"

Forty-five minutes later, Mia found herself checking into a hot, musty, generic motel room out at the interstate. Dylan had tried hard to get her to spend the night upstairs above the bar. But she needed some space and distance to weigh the pros and cons of his unexpected offer. He had the uncanny ability to make people see things his way. She wanted to be sure she was considering all the aspects of his proposal before she gave him an answer.

The pluses were obvious. Time with her daughter. An

immediate paycheck. No need to look for a new place to live when her lease ran out in a week. And it wasn't as if she had a lot of other appealing choices. She would get a job in the Raleigh/Durham area eventually, once she found another lab looking for her set of skills. If she were lucky, the employer might even offer on-site, discounted day care. She knew of several companies that did so. But tracking down such a position would take time—time when she wasn't bringing in money and didn't have a place to live.

Or if she agreed to work for Dylan, she would have a roof over her head, food to eat and more time with Cora while she looked for employment in her field. Only a fool would say no—right?

Then why was she hesitating?

It all came down to Dylan. It was one thing for a young girl to have a crush on a popular senior jock. That was practically a rite of passage. But as Dylan had pointed out, Mia was all grown up. And her reactions to the equally grown-up Dylan were alarming.

The times she had tried dating in her adult life had been either disastrous or disappointing. Until she walked through the doors of the Silver Dollar Saloon, she had honestly thought she didn't have much of an interest in sex or men. But coming face-to-face with Dylan exposed the lie she had told herself for years.

Dylan wasn't a high school crush. He was the boy, now the man, who had made her aware of her sexual self. His masculine strength and power made her feel intensely *female*. In every other area of her life, people looked at her as a *brain* first and foremost.

She did valuable work. She knew that. Her intelligence had led her to projects and challenges that were exciting and fulfilling. But sometimes it felt that she could have just as easily been a robot. No one cared that she had emotions or, heaven forbid, *needs*.

That wasn't *entirely* fair. Janette was a dear friend. And Janette was the one who'd introduced Mia to Howard, the botany professor who dated Mia for six months, courted her circumspectly and eventually shared her bed. Their relationship had been comfortable and undemanding, laden with pleasant conversation as well as shared interests and backgrounds.

But in the end, the absence of sparks between them meant a sad, inevitable breakup due to lack of sizzle.

With Dylan, there was plenty of sizzle—an entire forest fire of sizzle. Not necessarily on his part, but definitely on Mia's. All she had to do was look at him and she remembered exactly how she had felt as a girl of fifteen. Perhaps the tutoring had erased some boundaries between them. Or maybe because they had kept their relationship secret, it had felt safe to her. But whatever the reason, Dylan was the only male to make her feel this way.

Discovering that truth was disheartening. If she had let a teenage crush spoil her for other men, she was doomed to a single, celibate life. On the other hand, maybe she could make her obsession work *for* her, not against her. A hefty dose of exposure to the mature Dylan could prove to her that the boy she had idolized was just a guy like any other. She could flirt with him, maybe even sleep with him, and then go on her way.

She tucked Cora into the portable crib and sighed with relief when the baby actually curled into a ball and went still. Cora had fallen asleep on the ride over, but Mia had anticipated another long night of being up and down with her. Maybe Dylan had worn her daughter out.

Showering and changing as quietly as she could, Mia crawled into bed and yawned. She had promised Dylan an answer tomorrow. He had given her both the bar's number and his cell-phone number. But now she had more to think about. Her limbs felt restless and her body heavy. If she stayed in Silver Glen for six weeks, or maybe eight, however long it took to find another position suited to her skills and experience, would that be long enough to get Dylan out of her system?

Merely the thought of it made her breath catch and her thighs clench.

Janette hailed from Silver Glen as well. Though she was older than Mia, their hometown connection was what led them to become friends in Raleigh. Janette kept up with several family members in Silver Glen, and it had been a source of hot gossip when Dylan's engagement to a young starlet ended abruptly a few years ago.

As far as Mia knew, Dylan had played the field since. If there was no one special in his life, she wouldn't have to feel guilty about using him for her own personal entertainment.

Maybe if she could work up the courage to let him know what she wanted, they could have a mutually satisfying sexual relationship, and then as soon as Mia got a job, she and Cora would move back to Raleigh.

Cora was sleeping, but Mia was not. Her pulse jumped and skittered. Her breath came in short bursts. The exhilaration she experienced was couched in incredulity and terror. What on God's green earth led her to think she could seduce any man, much less the gorgeous Dylan Kavanagh?

Before she could lose her nerve, she reached for her cell phone on the bedside table. Hands trembling, she sent a text. I'll do it. But only until I get a job in my field. Working for you will be strictly temporary. As she hit Send, she wondered whom she was trying to convince.

Ninety seconds passed before he responded. Had he been sleeping? Imagining him naked and warm beneath a thin sheet made her hot enough to toss back the covers.

A quiet ding signaled his answer.

Good. Need help moving?

No. Friends will help me pack or keep the baby. When should I come?

A week? Ten days? The sooner the better. I'm drowning in ledgers.

If you find somebody else in the meantime, let me know.

I don't want anybody else. I want you.

Four

As soon as Dylan hit Send, he groaned. That last text could be misconstrued. But surely the prim and proper Mia wouldn't read it that way. All he had in mind was repaying Mia for what she had done for him so long ago. Any man worth his salt knew that an honorable guy settled his debts.

He'd thought about Mia over the years, usually with guilt for the way he had treated her. Sure, they had ended up being friends before it was all over, but it had been a clandestine bond. He'd been too macho and too ashamed of his academic weaknesses to let anyone see that he actually liked and respected a mousy little fifteen-year-old.

Even if his bookkeeper hadn't quit, he would have found some way to help Mia. He had lots of friends in town. But serendipity meant that not only did he really need Mia's help, but he was able to provide a place for her and Cora to stay rent-free. This arrangement was going to go a long way toward easing his conscience.

He turned over in the bed and sprawled on his stomach, feeling sleep struggle to claim him. At times like this, he envied his brother Liam. What would it be like to have the woman you loved tucked up in bed beside you every night? Zoe's effervescence was the perfect foil for Liam's serious side.

Dylan had heard his brother laugh more in the past few months than he had since they were kids. Liam was happier, less stressed, infinitely mellower. Even when it came to Liam, Dylan had guilt. When their father disappeared two decades ago, Liam, a mere lad of sixteen, had manned up to help their mother run the Silver Beeches Lodge, the extremely high-end hotel that had built their family finances.

While the rest of them were exploring options and making mistakes and generally learning what life was all about, Liam had stepped forward in a course already mapped out. He claimed not to resent his lot. He'd told Dylan more than once that running the hotel with Maeve Kavanagh was something he enjoyed.

Even so, Dylan hoped that Zoe would help Liam take care of a few items on his bucket list. His older brother was a hell of a guy, and he deserved the best.

Dylan sighed deeply, his body boneless as it succumbed to sleep. He'd have to paint the apartment before Mia came, and rearrange furniture to make space for the baby bed... and maybe even...

Fortunately for Mia, she wasn't a pack rat. Most of her belongings consisted of books and bookcases, kitchen items and clothes. With Janette's help, she spent one weekend boxing up most of the contents of her condo and ferrying it a bit at a time to a storage unit. She paid for three months in advance, knowing that surely by that time she would be back on her feet.

She still had her suspicions that Dylan was inventing work for her. His need to say thank-you, or do penance, was not something she took seriously. Anything she had done for him in the past had been freely offered. But she wasn't going to turn down the chance to have a safety net while she looked for a new job and to spend time with Cora. Eight weeks...twelve at the most. That seemed reasonable.

Having a shot at becoming one of Dylan's *flings* was merely a bonus. He was a man. She was a woman. All she had to do was get him to concentrate less on her IQ and more on her curves.

Cora, bless her, had been in a sunny mood most of the time, snoozing in her crib until it had to be dismantled. Janette's boyfriend offered to pick up the small U-Haul trailer Mia had rented. He insisted on hooking it to her SUV and helping her load everything that was going to Silver Glen.

By the time Mia pulled away from her building, waving at Janette in the rearview mirror, she was exhausted, but the sense of turning a new page in her life was infinitely preferable to the miasma of panic and failure that had dogged her the last month. All of her misgivings had dissipated. Returning to Silver Glen was going to be wonderful.

Five hours later, she turned onto the street where the Silver Dollar was located and hit her brakes to avoid crashing into a fire engine. In front of her, two white-and-orange barricades made it clear that she had reached the end of the road.

She rolled down her window and leaned out to speak to a uniformed cop. "What's going on?" She couldn't see far enough ahead to tell what had caused the commotion.

The cop shrugged. "Fire at the Silver Dollar, but they've got it under control now."

All the breath left her lungs. "Dylan?"

Her pale-faced distress must have registered, because he backpedalled rapidly. "No one hurt, ma'am. It happened early this morning. The building was empty."

She leaned back in her seat and tried to catch her breath. "I'm supposed to meet someone there."

The officer glanced in the backseat where Cora was

sucking enthusiastically on a pacifier. "At the bar?" His skepticism made her feel unaccountably guilty.

"Mr. Kavanagh has hired me to be his new bookkeeper. I'm moving into the upstairs apartment."

The man shook his head, sympathy on his weathered face. "Not today, you're not. I hope you have a plan B. The second floor is a total loss."

Dylan leaned against a lamppost, grimly studying what was left of his saloon. Thankfully, the main floor had sustained mostly smoke and water damage. But it would be quite a while before the Silver Dollar could reopen for business. He would pay his staff full wages, of course. But that still left the problem of his newest employee. And her child.

As he pondered his next steps, someone tapped him on the arm. When he turned, Mia stood looking at him, Cora clutched to her chest. "What happened, Dylan?" Her eyes were round.

"My own damn fault, apparently. It's been hot as Hades this last week, so I left the window AC units in the apartment running on high all night. I didn't want you or the baby to be uncomfortable today while you were getting settled. From what the fire marshal tells me, it looks like one of them shorted out and started the fire."

Mia turned to stare at the building, her expression hard to read. The scene still crawled with firefighters and investigators. No one wanted to take a chance that nearby structures might get involved.

Her shoulders lifted and fell. "Well, I guess that's that."

"What do you mean?"

"It means Cora and I will be driving back to Raleigh."

He heard the resignation in her voice. "Don't be ridiculous. Nothing has changed except where you and Cora will be sleeping. My house is huge, with more than enough room for guests."

Her chin lifted. "I'm not a charity case. It's out of the question."

For a moment he saw a spark of the temper he hadn't known existed. Perhaps Mia wasn't so meek after all. "I hired you in good faith. I'll sue for breach of contract if you leave."

Her eyes narrowed. "Don't be absurd."

"The building may be a mess at the moment, but I still have a business to run on paper."

"I'll have to find a place to rent until the repairs are finished."

"First of all, rental property in Silver Glen is slim pickings. And even if you found something, they'd want you to sign a twelve-month lease. You and Cora won't be here that long."

"You have an answer for everything, don't you?"

He had ruffled her feathers for sure. "It won't be so bad, I swear. My place is plenty big. I won't bother you at all."

"And what if the baby bothers you? What if she cries in the middle of the night?"

He grinned, feeling his mood lift despite the day's events. "I think I can handle it. C'mon, Mia. Think outside the box. We were friends once upon a time."

"I've changed. I don't let people push me around anymore."

"From what I remember, that was never the case with us." He shrugged. "If anything, you were the one ordering me to do this and that."

"I wouldn't have had to get tough if you hadn't been so stubborn."

"I've changed," he said, echoing her assertion and giving her his most angelic smile.

"I'll have to see it to believe it."

"Then that settles it. Let me get my car and you can follow me home."

"I never agreed to this nonsensical plan."

"But you know you're going to. in the end. From what I can tell, you're stuck with me for a few weeks. Chin up, Mia. It won't be so bad."

Mia knew Dylan Kavanagh was rich. Everybody knew it. But when you spent time with him, that knowledge tended to get shoved into the background. He had spent his life proving that he was just an ordinary guy. No flashy clothes. No Rolex watch on his wrist. No silver spoon.

The truth, however, was somewhat different. Mia had plenty of opportunity to chew on that fact as she followed Dylan's big, black pickup truck all the way outside of town and along a winding country road. When they turned off the main highway onto a narrow lane, weeping willows met overhead, creating a cool, green, foliage-lined tunnel that filtered sunlight in gentle rays.

Occasionally a pothole left over from the winter gave one of Mia's tires a jerk, but all in all, the road was in good repair. Cora slept through the trip, though soon she would be demanding to be fed. Thankfully, they rounded a bend in the road and Dylan's home came into view.

To call it a house would be like calling the Mona Lisa a finger painting. Dylan and his architect had created a magical fairy tale of a place. The structure, built of mountain stone, dark timbers and copper, nestled amidst the grove of hardwood trees as if it had been there forever. A small brook meandered across the front of the property. Someone had built a whimsical bridge over one section and a gazebo near another.

Flowers bloomed everywhere, not in any neat garden, but wild and free, as if they had claimed the space for their own. Mia rolled to a halt behind Dylan and turned off the car. She wanted to take in every wonderful detail, but Cora awoke as soon as the engine stopped.

Even now, Mia marveled that someone so small and perfect was hers to love. Except for getting her nights and days turned around, Cora was a very easy baby. She had already learned to smile and coo, and her pudgy arms and legs were the picture of health.

Try as she might, Mia couldn't see any evidence of traits from the anonymous man who had donated his sperm. Sometimes she felt guilty for robbing Cora of the chance to have a father, but other times she was simply happy to have a healthy child.

Dylan came back to help her with the diaper bag and the small suitcase that held immediate necessities. "You can have your pick of rooms," he said, ascending the wide stone staircase in step with her. "There are four bedrooms on the second story, but I'm sure you don't want to lug Cora up and down the stairs all the time. I think you'll like the guest suite on the main level. It has a small sitting room where you can put the baby bed, so you won't have to sleep in the same room with her."

As he opened the massive front door and ushered Mia inside, she almost gasped. The interior was straight out of an architectural magazine. Vaulted ceilings soared over the living area. Above them, a corridor with a fancy carved railing circled three sides. Doors opened off of it at regular intervals, presumably the bedrooms Dylan had mentioned.

On this level, however, the central open floor plan was flanked by wings to the left and right. "Kitchen, etcetera over there." Dylan pointed. "And in the opposite direction, two large suites."

Her cheeks heated. He was telling her that she and Cora would be staying in the wing that housed his quarters. She could ask for one of the rooms upstairs, but he was right.

Who wanted to carry a baby up and down the stairs for every nap and diaper change?

Cora began to whimper. Mia realized that feeding time couldn't be delayed much longer. Thankfully, Dylan was perceptive. He motioned toward the right side of the house. "If you go through the kitchen, you'll find a sunroom that has comfy chairs. It looks like she's getting hungry." He touched her head gently, stroking her silky hair. "She's been an angel, hasn't she?"

Mia nodded, feeling her breathing get jerky because he was so close. "It's actually easier to travel with her now than it will be in a few months. Once she's mobile, all bets are off."

His big body loomed over hers, his clothes smelling faintly of smoke, but not masking the aroma of shaving soap and warm male. Smiling, he cocked his head toward the opposite side of the house. "If you trust me to unload the trailer and set up the crib, I can get started on that while you're feeding her."

"I can't let you do all that," she protested weakly.

"Exactly how did you expect to hold an infant and unpack at the same time?" he asked.

"Quit being so damned logical." It had been a very stressful day, and it wasn't even dinnertime yet.

Dylan put an arm around her shoulders and steered her toward the kitchen. "It takes a village to raise a child— don't you know?" he said, grinning. "It wouldn't kill you to say 'Thank you, Dylan.'"

She sighed inwardly, feeling as if she were being railroaded, but not really having a choice at the moment. "Thank you, Dylan."

"That's better. Much better. Now go feed the kid before she gets any redder in the face. I'll handle all the rest."

Mia fell in love with the sunroom. It didn't really look like a Dylan room at all. At least not the Dylan she knew.

Cozy furniture covered in expensive chintz fabric beckoned a visitor to sit and fritter away a few hours. The windows were screened, so clearly when the temperatures allowed, they could be raised easily.

Bookcases lined the wall that bordered the hallway. Their presence gave her pause. Dylan had a long-standing battle with the written word, but maybe he had learned to enjoy some of volumes he had collected. In one corner of the room, a hammock suspended from a metal frame rocked slightly, as if propelled by an unseen hand. *Thou shalt not covet.* Mia remembered her mom's gentle admonition when she had wanted a shiny red bicycle like the one the girl next door owned.

Bicycles were one thing, but this room—oh, the temptation. Mia could see herself studying here, playing with Cora when she learned to crawl, perhaps knitting a sweater for someone she loved. In that instant, she realized that she had walked into danger.

Seeing Dylan every day in a business setting, even if it was a bar, would have been far less personal than staying in his house tucked away in the woods. Despite her silly fantasy of seducing him, she knew in her heart that the best course of action would be to keep her distance for however long she chose to stay in Silver Glen.

It was easy to imagine using him for a sexual fling, but she wasn't really that kind of woman. No matter how much she told herself she had come out of her shell, she wasn't in the category of females who took relationships in stride...who used sex as a game.

Case in point, her love life was so sterile, she'd chosen to conceive a baby with the help of an anonymous donor. That said louder than words she wasn't good at connecting with the opposite sex.

Sitting down and propping her feet on an ottoman, she settled Cora at her breast and gazed out over Dylan's backyard. It was a veritable Garden of Eden, filled with trees perfect for climbing. Why had he built such a house for himself? Did he plan to get married one day? Or had his aborted engagement soured him on the idea of wedded bliss?

It didn't really matter. The only thing Mia needed to know was that he was willing to play host to her and her baby until his building was repaired. At the rate of most home improvement projects, that could be well after Mia was gone.

Cora ate hungrily, her quiet slurping sounds making Mia smile. Even in the darkest moments when she had lost her job and her roommate had moved out and Cora had been wide-awake at three o'clock in the morning, Mia had not regretted getting pregnant, not at all. Being a mom was hard. But she had done a lot of difficult things in her life. Starting school at age four. Skipping two grades. Entering college at sixteen. Tutoring a moody boy with enough anger and testosterone to make a girl feel faint.

He had tried so hard to pretend that he didn't care. But Mia had known. Dylan hated feeling stupid. He resented needing her help as much as he'd been relieved to have it.

Maybe this arrangement would give him some kind of closure. Seeing Mia's predicament should reassure him that intelligence was no buffer against the difficulties of life. No matter his challenges as a youth, he had far surpassed what many people had thought him capable of accomplishing. Even without the backing of his wealthy family, Mia was convinced that Dylan would have been just as successful. It might have taken him longer, but he would have gotten there eventually.

He had drive and determination and the kind of creativity that saw ideas and possibilities. Mia envied his fearlessness. It had taken her years to escape the prison of feeling socially inept and painfully shy.

Cora pulled away and looked up at her with bright eyes. Carefully balancing the baby on her knees, Mia buttoned her shirt and wondered whether to stay put or to seek out her host. "We're in uncharted waters, my little beauty."

Cora gurgled what might have been agreement. Mia put the baby on her shoulder and patted her back until a definite burp emanated from the tiny body. "Let's go find Dylan."

Five

Dylan gave the bed a shake to make sure it was steady. No squeaks. No wobbles. He plopped the mattress into place and stepped back to admire his handiwork. Printed instructions were often useless to him. Fortunately, he had a knack for three-dimensional reasoning that allowed him to construct almost anything that required wood and screws and nails.

"Wow, that was fast."

He turned and saw Mia and Cora staring at him with identical wide-eyed expressions. "It's not too complicated. But I didn't know where you'd packed the crib sheet. I put your three suitcases in the next room. I'm assuming the boxes can wait until morning?" He glanced at his watch. "I hate to be a poor host, but the fire marshal called to say I can come downtown now and go inside to assess the damage. And I promised some friends of mine we'd play pool at a buddy's house tonight. I can cancel, though...."

Mia straightened her spine, her arms wrapped protectively around Cora. "We don't need you to look after us. We'll be fine. Go. Do whatever you have to do."

As he drove away from the house a few minutes later, he told himself that the weird feeling in the pit of his stomach wasn't disappointment. Of course Mia didn't need him. This whole setup was for *his* benefit...so he could assuage some lingering guilt from high school. He was giving her a place to stay, sure. But she would more than earn her keep when she combed through the mess that was his bookkeeping system.

Dylan had tried to make sense of the various computer files. But in the end, he'd been nothing but frustrated. He suspected that he'd done more harm than good when he'd tried to enter recent debits and credits. Though he had learned to read for pleasure, it was a slow process. Numbers were a nightmare.

When he pulled up in front of the bar, the fire marshal waved him forward. "The upstairs is not safe to access, but you're welcome to take anything you need from the main level."

Dylan wrinkled his nose at the acrid odor of burnt wood. "My insurance company is in Asheville. They're sending someone out tomorrow."

"The numbers will add up. You'd be amazed at how much it costs to recover from water damage alone, much less the smoke."

"Yeah. But I'm more worried about the time. I'd like to reopen in a month. You think that's possible?"

The other man shook his head. "I don't know, Mr. Kavanagh. Money can grease a lot of wheels. But it's still a cumbersome process. Be careful in there. The floors are slick."

Dylan walked through the door of the Silver Dollar and groaned inwardly. The place over which he had labored so hard and so long was a wreck. He didn't have to worry about vandals. There was nothing much left worth stealing at this point.

His main objective was to recover anything Mia might need from his office. The small space smelled as bad as the rest of the building, but it wasn't as wet. Fortunately, he had a remote server at home that served as a backup for all his work files. His computer now stood in a puddle of water, so he didn't have much faith that it would reboot.

He found a cardboard carton that was mostly intact and scooped all the papers off the top of his desk. They could be dried out, and if worst came to worst, he'd ask vendors to resend their invoices.

This wasn't how he had anticipated getting reacquainted with Mia. He wanted to give her the impression that he was a solid businessman with an enthusiastic clientele. Instead, he was left with a smelly, sodden mess.

All in all, it could have been worse. At least the outer structure was intact. Since there was no rain in the forecast, he loaded everything into the back of his truck. He definitely didn't want that smell in the cab.

Over beer and burgers, his friends grilled him about the fire. They were equal parts sympathetic to his predicament and bummed out that their favorite watering hole was closed down indefinitely. Dylan managed to change the subject eventually, uncomfortably aware that several of these men barely managed to make ends meet from paycheck to paycheck. He didn't want anyone feeling sorry for him when all he had to do was throw money at his problem, and eventually it would resolve itself.

If the men sitting around the table ever resented the fact that his bank account ran to seven figures, they never showed it. But he had to wonder if his connection to the Kavanagh fortune at times made them uncomfortable.

Shaking off the odd sense that he didn't belong, he finished off his drink and stood. "Who's gonna be first in line for an ass-kicking at eight ball?"

When Cora went down for an early-evening nap, Mia snooped unashamedly. She'd put the baby monitor beside Cora's bed and carried the receiver in her pocket. That left her free to roam Dylan's gorgeous house at will. She started with the upstairs bedrooms. They were immaculately decorated and looked ready to welcome guests at any moment.

Despite that, they had an air of emptiness about them. Exactly how often did Dylan actually have overnight company?

His kitchen was a dream, especially the fancy appliances. Mia knew how to nuke anything, but the largesse in Dylan's refrigerator made her stomach growl. He'd told her his housekeeper kept him well stocked with food, but that was somewhat of an understatement. Mia found a freezer full of packages labeled with names like chicken parmesan, vegetable soup, whole-wheat bread. Added to what was in the fridge itself, she surmised that Dylan could easily hole up here and not go hungry for a month or more.

Since he had enjoined her to make herself at home and help herself to anything she wanted for dinner, she wasted no time in picking out what looked to be an individual serving of chicken potpie. While it thawed in the microwave, she glanced at the monitor, making sure Cora was still asleep. The little girl was in her favorite position, with her butt lifted in the air and her knees pulled beneath her.

Shadows fell as Mia ended her meal. She would have to wake the baby up soon or Cora would never sleep tonight. Although Mia was not particularly anxious about staying alone, the house did seem bigger and emptier with dark on the way. She wondered how long Dylan would stay out.

None of her business, she reminded herself. If the original plan had worked out, she and Cora would be alone in the apartment over the bar. But at least the people and the noise would have kept her company until closing time.

Cora was in her usual sunny mood when Mia got her up. Somewhere in the car there was a plastic storage box with the baby's bathtub and other important items, but Mia decided to do without them tonight. She put Cora in the sink and managed to bathe her quickly before the odd circumstances could unsettle the infant.

Smelling like lotion and clean baby, Cora wriggled as her mother tucked her into pajamas. For an hour, they played on the king-size bed that was to be Mia's for the next several weeks. If Mia listened occasionally for the sound of a vehicle coming up the road, it was only because she was a little nervous about being so far out in the woods all alone.

It certainly wasn't because she was hoping to see Dylan again before she went to sleep.

Cora, for once, was cooperative when it came to bedtime. Her little eyelids drooped as Mia stood rocking her back and forth and singing one of the songs that was part of their bedtime ritual. When Mia laid Cora carefully in the bed, the baby wiggled for a moment and then curled her arms on either side of her head.

Turning out the light, Mia tiptoed backward out of the room and eased the door shut. Her heart jumped in her chest when she bumped into something big and warm. A hand came over her mouth, muffling her shriek.

"Easy, Mia. It's just me."

She struggled until he freed her. "You scared the heck out of me," she cried, glaring at Dylan as she tried to breathe normally.

"Sorry." He didn't seem overly penitent. "I thought you would hear me come in the front door, but you must have been busy with the baby. You want some ice cream?"

His prosaic question was at odds with the way his gaze roved over her body. She had changed into thin knit sleep pants and a spaghetti strap tank top. It was a perfectly respectable outfit for a hot summer night, even if it did reveal her nipples a tad too much.

"Ice cream would be nice," she said, crossing her arms over her chest. "Let me put a robe on."

His half smile made her knees quake. "Not on my account," he said. "I like you just the way you are. Follow me."

The house didn't seem nearly as big and threatening with the owner in residence. Mia sat down at the small table in the breakfast nook and watched as Dylan dished up enormous servings of praline pecan for each of them. Judging from the condition of his body, he clearly expended calories somehow, because there wasn't an ounce of fat on him anywhere.

He was lean and muscular. Physical power was on display, but restrained. Dylan was the kind of man a woman would want at her side if she were lost in the wilderness.

Joining her at the table, he offered her a bowl. "Dig in."

After four bites, she put down her spoon. "You're staring at me."

"Sorry." He leaned forward and wiped a smudge of caramel off her chin. "I'm still trying to match the grown-up Mia to my memories of a young girl."

His touch rattled her. "I'm surprised you remember anything at all about me. You were a senior, an exalted star, and I wasn't even in the same orbit."

"You were a senior, too," he pointed out, studying her as he licked his dessert off the back of his spoon.

She had never before seen anything sexy about eating ice cream, but Dylan was in a class by himself.

"I wasn't a *real* senior," she said, remembering the taunts and ostracism. The pecking order in high school was rigid and unbending. The fact that she was only fifteen years old and about to get her diploma was a sore spot for many of her classmates struggling to pass required courses.

"You had a hard time, didn't you?" In his eyes she saw dawning adult comprehension of what her life must have been like. "I'm sorry, Mia."

She shrugged. "I was used to it. And besides, I was neither the first nor the last high-school kid to be bullied. It could have been a lot worse. I always wondered if you had something to do with the fact that after Christmas, a lot of the kids suddenly changed toward me. They weren't exactly nice, but they weren't outright hostile anymore. Did you say something?"

"I might have. A bunch of us went on a ski trip over New Year's weekend. A couple of the jocks were talking about getting you in bed to prove that they could. I shut them down. That's all."

She paused, her spoon halfway to her mouth. "Why, Dylan Kavanagh...you were looking out for me." The knowledge gave her a warm fuzzy feeling.

His quick grin made him look more like the kid from high school. "Don't make me out to be a hero. I'm well aware that I gave you plenty of grief."

"And yet you kissed me once."

The words tumbled out of her mouth uncensored. She froze, aghast that she had dropped a conversational bomb.

Dylan was shocked that she had brought it up. And vaguely uncomfortable. He'd wondered if she even remembered the spring night right before they graduated.

"I never should have done that," he muttered, taking another bite of ice cream and hoping she didn't notice that his face had flushed. Even now, he could remember the taste of her lips.

But she had been fifteen, her sixteenth birthday still two months away, and he had been a man of eighteen by that time. His awkward embrace and quick, furtive kiss had felt both deliciously sweet and at the same time terribly wrong.

Mia set her spoon in her empty bowl and propped her

chin on her hand. "I always wondered why you kissed me. Was it a dare?"

"No. Hell, no." The idea was insulting. That would have made it even worse. "I had the urge, that's all. We'd been together all year, more hours than I cared to admit, and we were getting ready to graduate. Probably never going to see each other again, since you were headed off to school at some brainiac university."

"You can't tell me the Dylan Kavanagh I knew back then was sentimental. Try again."

"You were pretty in the moonlight," he said flatly. "I went to get something from the concession stand and there you were." They'd both, separately, been at Silver Glen's one and only drive-in theater. The place was in business even today. The owners were careful to keep it in good shape and to hire off-duty police officers for the premises so parents would still let their kids go there.

"You were with a date, weren't you?"

How could big dark eyes make him feel like such a heel? "Yes."

"So again...I have to ask. Why?"

"Damn it, Mia, I don't know." He stood and took his bowl to the sink, dropping it with a clatter. "You fascinated me. And intimidated me."

Her jaw dropped. "That's the most outrageous thing I've ever heard you say. You hated me for a long time. And after that you barely tolerated me."

"Not true." He leaned against the counter, his hands propped behind him on the sink. "I never hated you. It may have seemed that way in the beginning, but it was really myself I hated. You just caught the fallout. I may have acted like the biggest horse's ass ever, but I thought you were sweet and impossibly complicated."

She looked at him as if he had grown horns and a tail.

"Why won't you tell me the real reason you kissed me, Dylan?"

Fed up with her stubbornness and her utter lack of faith in her appeal, he strode to the table and grabbed her wrist, pulling her to her feet. "I kissed you because you made me hard and I dreamed about you most nights." Without thinking about the ramifications or the consequences, he lowered his head, muttering softly as he brought his lips close to hers. "You were an angel to me, the one and only person who could rescue me from the mess that was my life."

He came so close to kissing her, he could taste it. But Mia was rigid in his embrace. For about thirty seconds. Then something unexpected struck him in the chest and spread throughout his body. It was a feeling like being caught in a summer rain, drenched to the skin and laughing because it felt so good.

She hugged him. Her technique was awkward and tentative. The very lack of confidence in the way she responded stole beneath his defenses and swamped him with tenderness. She was not a young girl anymore. She was a grown woman with a soft body and full breasts and curvy hips that begged for a man's touch.

Much longer, and he'd be tempted to take her standing up. *Bad idea, Dylan.* He backed away reluctantly, breaking the physical connection though he couldn't deny a less tangible link that bound them together.

Mia stared up at him with an expression that was impossible to define. "You almost kissed me," she said.

He shrugged. "I thought better of it. You didn't believe me about that night at the drive-in, but it's true. I had a little bit of a forbidden crush on you back then."

"Forbidden?"

"You were too young, even if we *were* in the same grade. I may have been a hormonal teenage boy, but I knew you were off-limits."

"I was headed to college, same as you."

"Didn't matter. You were a kid, a very pretty, not-old-enough-to-be-legal kid."

"Am I supposed to be grateful that you kept your hands to yourself?"

He might not be the smartest man in the world, but he knew a pissed-off woman when he heard one. "What do you want from me, Mia?"

She was silent for so long, he began to sweat. And when she spoke she didn't really answer his question. "If we're being honest here, I suppose I should tell you that I didn't happen upon the Silver Dollar by chance."

His eyebrows went up. "You didn't?"

"No. I wanted to see you, and it wasn't hard to find out that you owned the saloon."

"You couldn't have known about the job, so why did you come?"

Mia sat back down, resting her elbows on the table and putting her face in her hands before she looked up at him with a crooked smile. "I've screwed up just about every aspect of my life. At the moment, I'm a homeless single mom with a helpless baby and limited funds. I thought it might make me feel better if I could be sure that *you* were doing well…that the tutoring I did in high school meant something. So I came back to Silver Glen for a visit."

"How did you know I would sit down at the bar and speak to you?"

"I didn't. But it wouldn't have mattered if we never came face-to-face. I could see right in front of me what you had created. A thriving business. People eating, drinking, having fun. Camaraderie. You're a success, Dylan. And that makes me feel good."

Six

Mia almost regretted her honesty. Dylan's visible discomfort was not the reaction she had expected. But he responded gruffly, "I'm glad."

"Don't get me wrong," she said quickly. "I'm not taking credit for your success. That's all you. But in high school you were at a critical juncture, and I like to think I helped...at least a little."

"Of course you did." He glanced at the clock on the wall. "If you have everything you need, I think I'll turn in. Whenever the baby naps tomorrow, you and I can go over the books, and hopefully you can get started when time permits."

The switch from personal to business gave her mental whiplash. Had Dylan been offended by what she said? Perhaps he thought she was presumptuous to pat herself on the back. Maybe the feeling she was trying to express had come out all wrong. "Dylan, I didn't mean that you couldn't have done it without me. That's not what I was saying."

He shoved his hands in his pockets, the line and angles of his face set in stone. "But it's true, isn't it? Without your help, I would have flunked out of high school. And when I dropped out of college, if my family hadn't had money I would have ended up flipping burgers at a fast-food place."

"That's crazy, I—"

He strode out of the room so quickly she was caught off guard. Running to catch up, she followed him across the huge, open living area. Just before he reached the wing where their bedrooms were located, she grabbed his sleeve. "Listen to me, Dylan. Your money isn't what made the saloon a success. It's you. The way you draw people together. Everybody loves hanging out at the Silver Dollar because you've made it comfortable and fun. Do you know how much I wish I had your gift for reaching people?"

He stopped. Not much choice, really, with her hanging on to his arm. But his face softened. "Still trying to save me from myself, Mia?"

"You don't need saving," she insisted. "But that chip on your shoulder must be getting hard to carry."

He ignored her deliberate provocation. "I'm meeting with the insurance adjustor at ten tomorrow. I should be back sometime after lunch. We can work on the bookkeeping stuff then. My housekeeper will be here in the morning. Please make yourself at home."

Before she could respond, he disappeared into his suite of rooms and closed the door firmly behind him.

Mia stood, nonplussed, and felt a rush of mortification. She shouldn't have brought up the past. Clearly it was still a sore spot. But it baffled her that no one else saw this side of Dylan. At the saloon, the customers related to him like he was a rock star, the women giggly and starry-eyed and the men standing a little straighter and pulling in their beer guts in an attempt to emulate the man whom everyone admired.

Dylan, by every definition, was a success in life, both professionally and personally. Despite his aborted engagement, he had surrounded himself with a wide circle of family and friends. Someday there might be a woman lucky enough and smart enough to snag him for a husband.

Turning and tiptoeing into her suite so as not to wake

the baby, Mia crawled into bed and turned out the light. In the dark, and in a strange place, she heard all sorts of pops and creaks as the house settled for the night. To take her mind off the unfamiliar noises, she imagined what Dylan might be doing. Perhaps he had showered and walked nude back into his bedroom. It was safe to imagine that a man like him slept in the buff. Just thinking about it made Mia shiver.

Sex with the professor had been unexceptional. Unlike Indiana Jones, Mia's short-lived lover had a body almost as soft as a woman's. The most physical thing he ever did was lift his arm as he wrote on the dry-erase board. Surely she wasn't so shallow that she had to have rock-hard abs and spectacularly defined muscles to get turned on.

A more likely and more palatable explanation was the fact that Dylan had stolen a piece of her heart when she was fifteen, and she had never gotten it back. She was an adult woman now. With needs. Needs that went beyond the necessity of finding a job or a place to live.

Sometimes at night, she lay in bed imagining what it would be like if she had a husband tucked in beside her, a soul mate to share the ups and downs of being a parent. It wasn't that she was afraid to work hard. She would do anything to ensure Cora's happiness and well-being. But even so, single parenting was lonely.

She didn't regret getting pregnant. Cora was a gift unlike any she had ever received in her life. Perhaps she was overthinking her decision. In the end, it didn't really matter if she had chosen a less-than-perfect route to motherhood. The deed was done. She had a baby. And the two of them were a family.

Moments later, hovering on the edge of sleep, deliciously drowsy and comfortable in Dylan's luxurious guest bed, Mia groaned when she heard the unmistakable sound of her daughter's cry.

Dragging herself upright on the side of the bed, she scraped her hands through her hair and rubbed her temples. Judging by the experience of past nights, she had about sixty seconds to pacify her baby before Cora launched into full-scale squalling. With a deep breath and a prayer for patience, she headed for the adjoining room, wondering if she would ever again get a full night's sleep.

Dylan heard Cora cry out. His first instinct was to get up and go see if he could help. But that seemed uncomfortably intimate in light of the fact that he and Mia had barely reconnected after not seeing each other for a dozen years. He had certainly never anticipated having her live in his house.

The truth was, he could more than afford to put her up at a hotel. Hell, his family owned the swank, exclusive Silver Beeches Lodge on top of the mountain. The hotel was no place for a baby, though. Not only might the other guests complain, but Mia and Cora needed privacy and space to be comfortable. He had more than enough room. One slip of a woman and her tiny infant were hardly likely to cramp his style, and besides, part of him wanted them close by.

He turned over in bed and lay on his stomach, his face buried in one arm. The air-conditioning was set at the usual temp, but he felt hot and restless. It had been too long since he'd slept with a woman. Seeing his brother's happiness made him jealous.

There…he'd admitted it. Which made him a pathetic lowlife. Knowing that his own engagement had crashed and burned when the woman he'd loved decided Hollywood had more to offer than Dylan Kavanagh had been a blow to his heart and his ego. He didn't begrudge Liam his happiness. Not at all. His older brother deserved every ounce of joy he'd found in the exuberant Zoe.

But Dylan's failure in the relationship department made him wonder if his judgment about women was as screwed up as his perception of numbers and letters.

Self-pity was a disgusting emotion. Normally, he spent little time bemoaning the defection of his fiancée, or even the fact that his reading comprehension sucked even now. But getting to know Mia again, on top of seeing the business he'd worked so hard to establish going up in smoke, had rattled him.

Tomorrow morning he'd get his head on straight. Tomorrow morning he'd make a fresh start in more ways than one.

In the meantime, surely it wasn't hurting anyone if he imagined what Mia Larin looked like all grown up. And naked.

When light filtered into Mia's room, she wanted to pull the covers over her head and pretend that it was still the dead of night. Cora had played on Mia's bed, cooing and clutching a rattle, until almost one in the morning when she finally wore herself out and fell asleep. Mia had laid her daughter gently in her crib, returned to her own room and been comatose almost instantly. The baby awakened at five for her usual feeding, but thankfully, had gone right back to sleep.

Mia felt sluggish and hungover, which really wasn't fair since she hadn't consumed so much as half a glass of wine since the first day she decided to get pregnant. Before launching on her solo adventure, she had read book after book about nutrition, ovulation, maternal health and mental preparation. Given the repeated disappointments she had weathered as the months passed, there had been more than one occasion when a good, stiff drink might have helped.

Rolling onto her side, she glanced at the clock. The

thought of another hour's sleep sounded like heaven, but her stomach rumbled, and she knew that once Cora was up, Mia's morning meal would consist of little more than a banana eaten standing up and a cup of coffee.

Ever so quietly, she dressed in jeans and a yellow cotton shirt that buttoned up the front. Maybe the cheery color would help cut through the fog of sleep deprivation.

Though she had never exactly been a fashion icon, her wardrobe lately tended more toward practical than stylish. Though she would have liked to appear trendy and put together for Dylan's benefit, it probably wasn't going to happen. Lately, more often than not, she noticed halfway through the day that Cora had spit up on her shoulder. Not exactly the way to entice a man.

With the baby monitor tucked in her pocket, Mia crossed the living room in her bare feet, making a beeline for the kitchen and the smell of coffee. Though Dylan had warned her his housekeeper would be in residence this morning, it was still somewhat of a shock to come face-to-face with an angular woman whose short-cropped gray hair—along with a black uniform—gave her a stern look. Mia judged her age to be between sixty-five and seventy.

"Oh," Mia said, pulling up short. "I'm Mia Larin. And you must be Dylan's housekeeper."

When the woman smiled, her entire demeanor transformed. "That's me," she said. "My name's Gertie. What can I get you for breakfast, dear?" Without asking, she poured a cup of coffee and pressed it into Mia's hand, pointing out the sugar and creamer on the table.

Mia shook her head. "Please don't think you have to wait on me. I'm here to work for Dylan. In fact, I was supposed to be living above the bar, but, well…you know what happened."

Gertie grimaced. "A damn shame. But Dylan will put it to rights. That boy never loses sight of a goal. And by the way, my job is to take care of Mr. Kavanagh and his guests. He specifically asked me this morning to make sure you and the baby were settled in. So no back talk from you, young lady." Her smile indicated that she was joking, but Mia had a feeling that crossing Gertie wouldn't be a good idea.

"Well, in that case, I'd love some toast and one of those grapefruits over there."

Gertie hunched her shoulders and scowled. "You nursing?"

It was a rather personal question from someone she had just met, but Mia answered anyway. "Yes, ma'am." She'd been brought up to respect her elders. Despite Gertie's position as housekeeper, Mia felt deference was in order.

"Then you need more food than that. You like your eggs scrambled?" At Mia's nod, Gertie turned toward the refrigerator. "Newspaper's on the counter. I know you young people get the headlines on your fancy phones or whatever, but in my opinion, nothing gets the day off to a good start like reading the comics and the obituaries over a decent cup of coffee."

Mia, somewhat chastened, picked up the copy of the *Asheville Citizen-Times*. "Dylan subscribes to this?"

Gertie snorted. "No. I bring my copy from home. But I've caught him checking his stocks a time or two."

"Have you worked for him very long?"

"Ever since he built this house. So, I suppose we're closing in on three years or so."

That answered the question of whether or not Dylan had put down roots when he fell in love. The engagement had been longer ago than that, so he must have broken ground for this amazing house simply because he wanted a place of his own.

Mia pretended an interest in the paper, but she was more enthralled in watching Gertie. The older woman moved about the kitchen with an economy Mia admired. Mia rarely cooked, and when she did, the results were never the same. She knew how to read a formula and how to follow rules. But somehow, her culinary efforts always fell short. Perhaps she could pick up a few tips while she was here.

In no time, Gertie set a plate of eggs, sausage and biscuits in front of Mia, flanked by a small bowl holding a perfectly sliced and sectioned grapefruit half. "Thank you," Mia said. "This looks delicious."

"It is." Gertie's grin was smug. "Mr. Dylan likes a clean house, but he didn't hire me 'cause I know how to vacuum. That boy loves his food."

"You'd never know it to look at him." Mia's face flamed, realizing that it probably wasn't good form to exhibit such oblique though obvious appreciation of her landlord's physical attributes.

Gertie merely chuckled. "He burns it off. Never sits still that I can tell. How do you two know each other?'

"We were in school together."

"Ah." Gertie washed the iron skillet she'd used to fix Mia's eggs and dried it with a paper towel. "Mr. Dylan told me you're going to be doing the books for him. I want you to know that I'd consider it an honor to take care of the baby whenever you ask."

Mia gaped. "Well, uh…"

"Oh, you can trust me, honey. I've got five kids of my own and twelve grandchildren. Don't get to see them as much as I'd like. They're spread all over the country. But I'm good with babies."

"That's a lovely offer," Mia said faintly, feeling a bit overwhelmed. "I'm sure it will take me a few days to get into the swing of things, but I'll keep that in mind."

"I'd do anything for Mr. Dylan."

There was a certain level of fervor in the terse statement that begged for a question. "Because he pays well?"

"No." Gertie paused. "Well, yes, he does. But that's not what I meant. Mr. Dylan helped me out of a tight spot once, and I owe him."

Mia wasn't nosy as a rule. And she certainly wasn't assertive in situations like this. But Gertie seemed primed to share information. "How so?"

The housekeeper poured herself a cup of coffee, leaned against the counter and took a sip. Black. No sugar. "One of my grandsons came to live with me three summers ago. He'd been raisin' hell back home and his momma and daddy thought a change of scenery would do him good. But the little weasel brought drugs with him here to Silver Glen and tried to sell them. Sheriff caught him and tossed him in jail. I had to bail him out."

"So Dylan loaned you the money?"

"I had the money. It wasn't that. But I'm an old woman. A fifteen-year-old boy with an attitude won't take advice, even from me. Dylan hauled his butt out of jail and gave him a tongue-lashing for upsetting his grandmother. The boy had a choice between doing jail time, going home to his momma and daddy or working for Dylan all summer."

"I'm assuming he chose Dylan?"

"Sure did. In ten weeks, Mr. Dylan talked more sense into that hardheaded rascal than the rest of us put together. The kid looked up to him, and the lectures came easier from his mentor than from me or his parents. My grandson is in college now. Making straight As. And he hasn't touched drugs since he left Silver Glen. Mr. Dylan did that."

Mia ate her breakfast in silence, her respect for Dylan growing. Perhaps because he'd been such a hell-raiser himself, he understood the mind-set of a rebellious teenage boy. Not that Dylan had ever dabbled in drugs. He'd been a sports fiend, determined to keep his body in top physical shape. But he had definitely taken pride in flouting authority.

It didn't take a psychologist to see that Dylan had been compensating for his struggles in the classroom. It was no help that his older brother, Liam, had breezed through high school and gone on past college to get an advanced degree.

Sibling rivalry at that age was tough. Dylan must have felt the sting of not measuring up. So to prove he didn't care, he'd pulled stunts like kidnapping Mr. Everson's prize bull and tying it to the flagpole in the center of town. Dumping a case of red food coloring and a gallon of detergent into the fountain in front of the bank. Snitching the principal's ugly burgundy blazer and literally running it up the flagpole.

No one was ever harmed by Dylan's pranks. And he was usually the one who had to pay the price for cleaning up his messes. But his antics had worked. In Silver Glen High School, by the time Dylan reached his senior year, he was the most popular guy around, hands down. Mia had been an invisible nobody.

She finished the last bite of her lighter-than-air biscuit and pushed back from the table. "That was wonderful, Gertie. Thank you so much."

"Glad you enjoyed it. Lunch will be ready at twelve-thirty, as long as Mr. Dylan makes it back from town. Anytime you need washing done for you or the baby, just drop it on the floor in the laundry room."

"Oh, but I—"

Gertie held up a hand. "It's my job. *Your* job is to look after the baby and the books. Don't be tryin' to wash dishes or mess around in my kitchen. This is my turf. And I'm going to make your life easier, because that's what Mr. Dylan wants."

Seven

Dylan had a good news/bad news kind of morning. On the upside, he had very good insurance. The financial hit wasn't going to be too bad at all. But in the negative column was the fact that the contractor he wanted to do the renovation couldn't start for three weeks. In other words, hurry up and wait.

He swallowed his impatience as best he could. Sooner or later the bar would reopen, and he was confident that his regulars would return. Nothing could be done about the lost business in the meantime.

When he was satisfied that he had taken care of the essential details to get the ball rolling with the adjustor and the repair work, he jumped in his truck and headed for home. Knowing that Mia and Cora would be there when he arrived was another item for the plus column.

He found his houseguests in the sunroom. Pausing in the doorway, he absorbed the picture they made. Mia was down on the carpet, stretched out on her side. Where her yellow top buttoned near her waist, one side of the fabric gaped, giving him a tantalizing glimpse of pale white skin. Cora lay on a fuzzy pink blanket, kicking her legs and rolling from side to side as Mia laughed softly. "It won't be long, sweet pea."

"Won't be long until what?" Dylan strolled into the

room and sprawled into his favorite recliner that just happened to be at Mia's elbow.

She sat up and straightened her clothing, her cheeks flushed, either from playing with her daughter or because seeing Dylan flustered her. "Until she rolls over completely. The doctor says Cora's at the top of the charts physically."

"You may have an athlete on your hands."

Mia shook her head. "Not if she has my genes. I was lucky that my high-school gym classes were pass/fail, or my grade point average would have suffered. I've been known to trip over my own feet."

"That's only because your super impressive brain is tied up with loftier matters."

She gazed at him askance. "Are you making fun of me, Kavanagh?"

He reached down and tugged her ponytail. "Maybe. What are you going to do about it? I'm bigger and faster than you."

She scooped Cora into her lap and nuzzled her head. "I like the grown-up Dylan."

Her non sequitur caught him off guard. "What does that mean?" It sounded like a compliment, which made him suspicious. The Mia he had once known would never have been confident enough to flirt with a guy, even one she felt comfortable around.

"It means that I'm impressed with the man you've become. You're not angry anymore. And not out to prove anything, at least I don't think so. Some people would have been apoplectic after the fire yesterday, but you've handled it all so calmly."

The praise made him oddly uncomfortable. "Believe me, Mia, I'm nothing special. I have the luxury of a safety net. Not everyone is so lucky. It's not like I'm going to be destitute and on the street if the Silver Dollar goes belly-up."

She frowned. "Do you think it will?"

"I hope not. The guy I trust to do the restoration can't get to me until three weeks from now. Which means a long wait until I can reopen. But I'm pretty sure my regulars will come back."

"I can't imagine that they wouldn't." She glanced at her watch. "We'd better head for the kitchen. I don't want to get my knuckles rapped with a ruler if we're late for lunch. I think I'm scared of Gertie."

"Her bark is worse than her bite." He extended a hand and helped Mia to her feet. Cora yawned hugely, making him laugh. "Maybe I'm prejudiced, but she's really cute. Did she sleep okay last night?" He had heard her only that one time, but he didn't know how long the baby had stayed awake.

"So-so."

"Do you mind if I carry her?"

Mia surrendered the baby without comment, walking ahead of him as they followed their noses to the appetizing aromas of Gertie's handiwork. Dylan enjoyed the feel of the infant in his arms. The smell of baby shampoo brought back good memories from his childhood. Cora was still young enough that having a stranger hold her wasn't alarming.

That first evening at the Silver Dollar, she had gone to him without protest, her big brown eyes and pink dimpled cheeks the epitome of a happy baby. Dylan wondered which, if any, of her anonymous male parent's traits she had inherited. Dylan wasn't sure where he stood on the whole nature/nurture thing. But his gut told him that what mattered most was the love a child received *after* birth.

In the kitchen, Gertie bustled about, shooing them to

seats at the table and pouring iced tea and lemonade to go along with the home cooked vegetables.

Mia's face lit up. "Food, real food. I've about had my fill of microwave dinners."

Dylan sat down with Cora in his lap, scooting his silverware out of the way when the baby predictably reached for a fork. "You won't go hungry while you're under this roof. Gertie is so good she could be on one of those reality cooking shows."

Gertie turned bright red. "Oh, hush, Dylan. You're exaggerating."

At that very moment, Mia realized that the housekeeper loved her boss like a son. It was cute actually. The woman obviously doted on Dylan, and he treated her with a mixture of respect and affection that was very sweet to watch. He would probably hate knowing Mia thought anything about him was sweet. He might not *need* to prove he was a bad boy anymore, but there was nothing overtly soft about him.

He exuded masculinity effortlessly. It was in the way he walked and in the breadth of his shoulders and in the low rumble of his laughter. This Dylan might be older and more sophisticated than the boy she had known in school, but beneath the skin he was still a rough-and-tumble guy.

With Dylan behind the bar at the Silver Dollar, there would be no need for a bouncer. He could probably corral a rowdy drunk with one sharp frown and a quick trip through the front door. Dylan had never initiated fights as a teenager, at least not that Mia remembered. But there was no doubt in her mind that he possessed the physical strength and agility to handle himself in any situation.

Back in high school, he had been on the wrestling squad for a little while. But though he was very good at the sport, he hadn't seemed to enjoy it the way he did football and baseball. Dylan liked being part of a team and thrived on the camaraderie of the locker room. His leadership skills were apparent even then.

As Gertie refilled Mia's glass, Mia wondered if the other two had noticed her silence. She had "checked out" for a few minutes thinking about Dylan. Somehow, he managed to clear his plate and have second helpings while still holding Cora in the crook of his left arm. The baby had actually fallen asleep.

Gertie cleared away the dishes and stopped at Dylan's elbow. "I know you two have business to discuss. Miss Mia, what if I take the baby for a walk in the backyard? I promise I'll keep her in the shade."

Dylan looked at Mia inquiringly. "It's up to you."

Mia nodded. "Of course. If you don't mind. And please call me Mia."

Gertie seemed pleased. Dylan handed Cora over to her so carefully that the baby never stirred. Mia realized ruefully that being spoiled was dangerously addictive. Suddenly, she had a beautiful, albeit temporary, home, and on top of that no need to cook or clean. She even had a built-in babysitter when needed. The change from desperate exhaustion to a return of her usual energy told her how much she had been struggling.

Once it was just the two of them in the kitchen, Mia cocked her head and smiled at Dylan. "You're a natural with kids. Do you think you'll want a big family someday? Another limb on the Kavanagh family tree?"

His face darkened and he got up from the table, turning his back on her as he poured himself a cup of coffee. "I don't plan to have children."

The words were curt. His tone of voice said *not up for discussion*. Mia, however, was so shocked she didn't pause to consider dropping the subject. "Why not?"

The glance he shot her over his shoulder was stormy.

"Because I might have a kid just like me. And I wouldn't wish that on anybody. No kid deserves to feel stupid."

The vehemence in his voice stunned her. "Is that why your engagement broke up? She wanted kids and you didn't?"

He faced her now, nursing the mug in his big hands. His face was wiped clean of expression, but there was turmoil in his gaze. "Having kids never even came up. We didn't get that far."

"Sorry," she muttered. Seeing the way he interacted with Cora told her that he would be a wonderful father.

He shrugged. "Anyone in town could fill you in on every titillating detail of my engagement and its ignominious end."

"Forget it. I shouldn't have asked. Why don't we get started looking at the saloon books?"

"Not yet. Obviously you're interested. And I've got nothing to hide. I fell for a cute blonde with a bubbly personality that nicely disguised a streak of ambition a mile wide."

"There's nothing wrong with having ambition."

"True. But it's not like I was planning to keep her barefoot and pregnant. The thing is, I was embarrassingly infatuated with her. Bought her a flashy engagement ring. Showered her with gifts. Maybe dating a movie star fed my ego, who knows?"

"I'm sure it was more than that."

"I never have been able to decide if it was my heart or my pride that took a hit. Doesn't really matter, though. She was here for three months filming a movie. When it was over, she had convinced herself that she loved the pace of life in Silver Glen, the sense of community and me."

"But she didn't."

"Let's just say that when her favorite director called

with an offer for the role of a lifetime, she hit the road so fast I never saw it coming."

"Surely you could have worked something out."

"She didn't want to. And in the end, that was probably for the best, because I belong in Silver Glen and she doesn't. She gave the ring back, kissed me with a tearful apology and left."

"I'm sorry, Dylan. That must have been a wretched time for you."

"It's worse in a small town. No place to hide."

His crooked smile tugged at her heartstrings. Mia couldn't imagine walking away from Dylan Kavanagh if he were in love with her. Clearly, the actress wanted success more than she wanted love. Or maybe she realized that whatever she and Dylan shared wasn't love at all.

"I hope I didn't bring back bad memories," she said.

It surprised Mia a little bit that she still felt so comfortable around him. Much like catching up with a cousin you hadn't seen in years, she and Dylan seemed to have picked up where they left off. But that analogy went only so far. There was nothing familial about her reaction to him.

"We all learn from our mistakes. Mine was a big one, but I've moved on." He took a cautious sip of coffee. "What about you? Is there a romantic debacle in your past?"

She sat back in her chair, enjoying the picture he made. Despite the fact that he leaned against the counter by the kitchen sink, there was nothing domesticated about him. He was a natural with children, but he didn't want any of his own. The knowledge made Mia sad.

The Kavanaghs had always seemed like a fairy-tale family to her. Despite the tragedy of losing Reggie Kavanagh, their close-knit relationships as they pulled together after his death fascinated an only child. As adults, the siblings probably had busy lives and didn't see each other as often as they liked. Maybe there were even sib-

ling rivalries that carried over into adulthood. But despite
any possible tensions, Mia envied them.

"I wouldn't call it a debacle," she said. "I dated a professor for a while. We had a lot in common, but not much
sizzle."

One corner of Dylan's mouth lifted in a sexy grin.
"Why, Mia. I didn't even realize you knew what sizzle
was."

"I'm neither a prude nor an innocent. Though I will
concede that my sexual experience compared to yours is
probably the equivalent of comparing miniature golf to a
professional game."

"Balls? Really? That's the metaphor you're going with?"

His wicked teasing shouldn't have rattled her. But he'd
always had the ability to throw her off-kilter. "Behave,"
she muttered. "If you know how." She stood and faced
him. "Shouldn't we get down to business?"

Dylan was somewhat perturbed that everything Mia
said sounded sexual to him. She wasn't doing it on purpose. At least he didn't think so. Maybe having a woman
sleeping in his house was not such a good idea. Too intimate. Too accessible. Too everything.

"The office is this way," he said gruffly.

Fortunately she followed him down the hall without
comment. Dylan's home office opened off the corridor
opposite the sunroom. He didn't spend much time there. It
was mostly a repository for business paperwork, because
at the saloon his walled "cubicle," as he liked to call it,
was much too small to house file cabinets. This room had
windows that let in the summer sun, and thick navy carpet that made a man want to go barefoot.

Today, however, he was the boss showing a new employee the ropes. As he glanced around the room, he felt
his neck flush. The place was a wreck. He hadn't realized

how bad it looked. Picking up a stack of *Sports Illustrated* magazines, he shoved several bunches of mail on top of them, attempting to clear a spot where Mia could work.

"Sorry," he said. He hadn't realized what a mess the room had become. "It's usually just me in here, so I don't bother much with cleaning."

Mia looked around with interest. "Don't worry about it. I'm sure you're always busy down at the bar. But I'd be happy to take a shot at organizing things a bit...if you trust me."

"Of course I trust you." He picked up a flat package that he had already opened with a knife and handed it to her. "I bought this to get you started."

Mia opened the carton and stared. "You got me a laptop?"

"It's top-of-the-line. And I had the guy at the computer store move all the files from the desktop at the Silver Dollar onto this baby. Fortunately, I had already dealt with that last week, because I think the old computer sustained some water damage."

Mia looked at the slim piece of technology with appreciation. "I've always wanted one so thin and light. Not that this one is mine, but it will be fun to use."

He pulled out the leather desk chair. "Sit down. Fire it up."

While he plugged in the power cord in case the unit wasn't fully charged, Mia opened the new toy and turned it on. When he stood from his crouched position on the floor beside her chair, her fingers were flying over the keys. "It's so fast," she said, her voice laden with excitement.

Rolling his eyes, he wondered if she had forgotten his presence. Testing a theory, he leaned forward and rested his forearms on the back of the chair. Now his head was close to hers, close enough that he could have kissed her

cheek if he had been so inclined. He hadn't really *stopped*
thinking about kissing her since last night.

She smelled good. The temptation was almost irresistible. But she was a guest in his home. His gut-deep need to
nibble the curve of her ear was inappropriate. He did touch
her hair, but so softly that he was sure she wouldn't notice.

Mia never flinched. "Where are the bookkeeping
files?" she asked.

"Everything you need is right here." He reached around
her and pointed to a tab. The faint, pleasing scent of her
perfume teased his nose. Her hair, tucked up in a ponytail
again, was silky and thick—the color of rich chocolate.
The urge to press his lips to the nape of her neck almost
shredded his resolve.

When her hands went perfectly still on the keyboard,
he knew she had finally realized that he was practically
embracing her. "Dylan?"

She turned her head and looked up at him. Without
analyzing it, he brushed the pad of his thumb across her
soft cheek. "What?"

Mia's small white teeth worried her lower lip. "I wondered when I accepted this job if we might become lovers."

He jerked upright so fast he practically cracked his
spine. It was one thing for him to try and rattle the sweetly
serious girl he had known in high school. Apparently this
new Mia was bolder. And apparently he wasn't as slick an
operator as he thought, because the light of interest in her
eyes threatened to knock him on his ass.

How had he lost control of the situation so quickly?

"That's not funny," he said. "Open one of those files
and let me show you how things work."

She swiveled her chair until she faced him. Her lips
twitched. "I'd like that. A lot."

"Stop it," he demanded.

"Stop what?"

"Acting like you want me to seduce you."

"I don't," she said simply, her hands now tucked primly in her lap. "I'm more interested in seducing *you*."

Maybe he had stepped through some kind of time warp into a parallel universe. It was the only explanation for this surreal conversation. He ran a hand across the back of his neck. "Are you trying to get back at me for being such a jerk in high school? Is that the reason for this charade?" She couldn't be serious.

Mia smiled sweetly. "You seem upset."

"I'm not upset, I'm just…" He trailed off, not quite able to articulate his feelings. It certainly wasn't unusual for a woman to come on to him. But Mia? Even in the midst of his consternation, his libido was at work, urging him to stop rationalizing and take advantage of the situation. "Maybe you're suffering from stress," he said desperately, reaching for any feasible explanation for her attitude. "Perhaps you should go lie down."

"Is that an invitation, Dylan?"

Eight

Mia wanted to laugh out loud at Dylan's hunted expression. He was the one who had touched her, not vice versa, but clearly he hadn't expected her reaction. Truthfully she was surprised at herself. When had she decided to reach for what she wanted? Both literally and metaphorically?

Perhaps trying so hard to get pregnant and finally succeeding had given her the confidence to face her fears. She had never had any trouble with academic challenges, but steering her personal life in a positive direction? That was a bigger hurdle to jump.

"Oh, forget it, Dylan," she said, keeping her tone light and teasing. "You're looking at me like I sprouted two heads. Your virtue is safe. Go away and let me get started on this."

The naked relief on his face was comical. "That's a good idea," he said heartily. "Having me here will be an interruption. That's my old bookkeeper's cell number there on the bulletin board. She said for you to call her anytime if you have questions."

The next thing Mia knew, she was alone in Dylan's office. His defection disappointed her. But she knew he was interested. The signs were all there. That *almost* kiss when they'd shared ice cream. His soft touch on her hair when he thought she didn't notice. He kept reaching out to her. She would give him time to get used to the idea.

Glancing at her watch, she realized that Cora would be ready to eat soon. Still, there was enough time to comb through the Silver Dollar's accounts-payable and accounts-receivable files. As she delved into her task, she saw that the computer program was straightforward. Her math skills were almost as strong as her language skills, so she soon felt confident that she could help Dylan.

That he would be helping her as well was a given.

By the time she shut everything down and went in search of her baby, Dylan was nowhere to be found. Gertie was sitting in the living room bouncing Cora on her knee. The baby was happy, but when she saw her mother, Cora wanted her.

Gertie handed Cora over with a smile. "Cute kid. Looks like you."

"Thank you for looking after her."

"Glad to do it."

"Is Dylan still around?"

"Nope. He lit out of here like a crazy man, mumbling something about a meeting in town. But it was the first I heard of it."

Mia grimaced inwardly. "I'm sure the fire has created a host of problems for him. Once I get the baby down for her afternoon nap, I plan to spend a couple of hours in the office seeing what things are urgent and which ones can wait. You don't have to cook for me if Dylan will be out. I'll be fine with a sandwich."

Gertie bristled. "Nonsense. You and the baby are my responsibility. That's what Dylan wants."

Dylan drove around town aimlessly. He couldn't go to work and he couldn't go home. That was a hell of a thing for a man to admit. Now that Pandora's box had been opened, all he could think about was what it would be like to have Mia Larin in his bed.

His fingers gripped the steering wheel as he broke out in a cold sweat. No good deed went unpunished. All he had wanted to do was give her—temporarily— a job and a place to live. To express his appreciation for what she had done for him in high school.

That was a noble goal. Right? So why was he hiding out? He was a man, damn it. Mia was a little mouse of a woman.

Except that she wasn't. Even as he said the words out loud, he knew they weren't true. Maybe Mia had been bashful and socially backward at fifteen, but definitely not now. She was a grown woman with goals and dreams. She'd wanted a baby, and she'd made it happen.

Was she serious about wanting Dylan?

Even as his body tightened at the thought, he acknowledged that it was a bad idea all the way around. Not on a physical level. Hell, he'd been on board with that since the moment he realized the grown-up Mia was a sensual, alluring woman.

But Mia didn't belong in Silver Glen, and he didn't want a woman getting close enough to him again to make him do something stupid. It didn't help that Mia had a beautiful little baby. The two of them together were a temptation he didn't need.

The idea of family and hearth and home had become more appealing to him in recent months. After his broken engagement, he had closed himself off emotionally. Aside from work, he was interested only in fun and games… having a good time. But after Liam and Zoe's wedding, some of the ice around Dylan's heart began to thaw.

Now he had brought two females into his home. Females who brightened up the place and gave it new life. So the temptation returned.

When his relationship with Tara ended, it had been tough. But there were no children involved. That experience had taught him a bitter truth. Either he picked the wrong women, or he himself wasn't very good in the relationship department.

Regardless, he was skittish about getting serious again. Especially with a woman who was already a parent. Dylan liked kids. No question there. But he doubted his ability to be the kind of parent who could nurture and care for a child of his own.

The only example he'd had growing up was Reggie, his feckless father. Dylan's dad was a Peter Pan at heart, always chasing the next crazy idea, leaving it to Maeve to do the lion's share of guiding seven boys. Dylan suspected he had inherited some of his dad's lack of focus. He'd be damned if he would ruin some kid's life.

Dylan had to keep reminding himself that Mia was passing through. Like his ex-fiancée, Mia would not be sticking around when the right job offer came along. Even if she *was* attracted to him, it was up to Dylan to be strong for both of them. Mia's defenses were down. She'd been through a grueling few weeks. An honorable man would not take advantage of that weakness. No matter how very badly he wanted to.

By the time he returned home in the late afternoon, he was certain he had a handle on the Mia situation. What he hadn't counted on was finding his mother, Maeve, sitting on his sofa conversing with his new houseguest. It wasn't entirely unheard of for his mom to drop by, but she usually called first. Maybe the gossipy grapevine had alerted her to Mia's presence. Maeve had been doing her best to play matchmaker for Dylan since the Tara incident.

Every one of his bachelor survival skills kicked into gear. "Hello, Mom. What brings you here?"

Maeve Kavanagh was an attractive woman in her early sixties. Her auburn hair with touches of gray, habitually kept in a bun, gave her an air of authority, but there was nothing matronly about her. Along with Liam, Maeve ran the Silver Beeches Lodge.

Dylan tossed his keys in a disk on the credenza by the front door and took a seat across from the two women. His mother cuddled Cora, a look of absolute joy on her face as she played with the baby.

Mia shot him a look that could have meant anything. "Your mother was worried about you. Because of the fire."

"I'm fine, Mom. But I appreciate your stopping by. Mia is staying with me for a bit. I guess you've already introduced yourselves by now. Do you remember her at all?"

Maeve tore her attention away from the infant long enough to frown at her son. "Of course I do. I thanked God for her every minute of your senior year. You were so busy being a rebellious adolescent that I couldn't get through to you, so I looked on Mia's assistance as a miracle."

Mia frowned. "It hadn't been that long since Dylan lost his dad. I think his behavior was understandable."

Dylan squirmed when his mother raised an eyebrow. He didn't need Mia defending him. Especially not to the parent who remembered all too well the many ways that he'd once tried to ruin his life. He stood, not caring if he was being rude. "I'll walk you out to the car, Mom."

Maeve grinned at Mia. "I believe that's 'Here's your hat, what's your hurry.' But since I do have a million things waiting to be accomplished, I'll go. It was lovely to see you again, Mia. I hope you'll join me for dinner at the Lodge one evening soon."

"Thank you, Ms. Kavanagh. I'd like that."

"As long as you bring the baby and call me Maeve."

Dylan escorted his mother out of the house, well aware he was about to get the third degree. What he hadn't expected was the way his parent looked at him with calculation in her eyes.

Opening her car door, but not getting in, she rested her arm on the frame. "Tell me the truth, Dylan. Is that baby yours?"

Startled shock tensed every one of his muscles. "Good God, Mother, no. I haven't seen the woman since high school."

"And yet she's tucked up nice and cozy in your house."

If anyone else, including his brothers, had subjected him to this line of questioning, he'd have told them to mind their own damn business. Unfortunately, that wasn't an option with his mother.

"Mia lost her job. I needed a bookkeeper. It's temporary. The plan was for her to live in the apartment over the saloon. Obviously, that's not an option right now."

Maeve's expression didn't change. "I don't want to see you get hurt. I don't want anyone taking advantage of your kind heart. You have this wonderful capacity for helping people, but it doesn't always serve you well in the end."

He stared down at the driveway, kicking a pebble with enough force to express his frustration. "You're talking about my ex-fiancée."

"Tara, the tramp, we call her. She used you, Dylan. It fed her ego to have a handsome hulk of a young man—a wealthy one at that—squiring her around town. I know the shape you were in when she left. You care, Dylan. Sometimes too much. Because people are not always what they seem."

"Mia's not like that. And the situations are totally different."

"I saw the way she looked at you when you walked into the room a moment ago."

He would have liked to argue the point, but given the surprising turn of events in his office earlier, he couldn't. "You have nothing to worry about. Mia's time here is very short. A woman with her qualifications and capabilities will have another job in no time."

"Bring her to dinner at the hotel. Zoe has been dying to cook for us in their suite."

Dylan's brother and his new wife lived on the top floor of the Silver Beeches Lodge, but they already had plans underway to build an incredible house. "I think being included in a family dinner would make Mia uncomfortable."

"Nonsense. I already invited her."

"She's nursing. I doubt she'd want to leave the baby for that long."

"Bring the baby with you. Maybe little Cora will give Liam and Zoe ideas. I'd like to be a nana before I have one foot in the grave."

"You never give up, do you?" He smiled, acknowledging the love and affection he felt for his mother. She had been widowed very young and yet managed to raise seven rambunctious boys and keep the family fortunes afloat. "I love you, Mom."

He kissed her cheek and tucked her into the car.

She stuck her arm out the window and waved a finger at him. "I'll check with Liam and Zoe and see what night works for them. No excuses."

Without answering, he watched her drive away. Hearing someone who cared so much about him put into words some of what he had been thinking sobered him. Was he susceptible to Mia simply because of auld lang syne and propinquity?

When he went back inside the house, he stopped to speak to the woman who had occupied his thoughts for most of the day. "Mia."

She looked up at him and smiled. "Your mother is sweet."

Dylan thought about that for a minute. Maeve had been

called headstrong and caring, but sweet? He squelched the instinct to plop down beside Mia and play with the baby, reminding himself of his recent resolve to keep them at a distance.

"I have several calls to make this evening, so I'm going to have dinner in my suite. You and Cora are welcome to make yourself at home anywhere in the house. I'll talk to you tomorrow."

I'll talk to you tomorrow.

But he didn't.

Mia was first surprised, then angry, then sad when she realized Dylan was making a concerted effort to be invisible. For five straight days, she never saw him nor heard from him. Gertie said he was hard at work tearing out the insides of the bar so that when the contractor was ready, the work could begin at once. None of which explained why a man with Dylan's fortune hadn't hired a crew to take over the dirty, smelly work. At night she caught sounds that might be him moving around in his room, but he came and went like a ghost.

It didn't take a genius to understand that Dylan was not going to follow up on her blatant invitation. Something inside Mia shriveled and died with the knowledge that for once in her life she had made the first move with a man, and now he was avoiding her as if afraid she might somehow jump him in his sleep. *Embarrassed* didn't begin to describe how she felt.

When she had been in residence almost a week, it became clear that she needed to be proactive about finding a *real* job. Living in Dylan's house was an untenable situation. The man was literally skulking around like a phantom because she had told him she wanted him.

Besides that, she needed to get back to work. As much as she adored Cora—and as lovely as it was to be waited on hand and foot—her brain needed the challenges it was accustomed to handling. The work she did was important. Her skills were a rare gift, one she could not in all good conscience fritter away.

One morning when Cora napped and after the records for the bar were in good shape, Mia used the laptop to write a new résumé. She'd been in her last job a very long time, so it wasn't hard to piece together her employment history.

Dylan had dangled the prospect of spending more time with Cora as an incentive for Mia to take the flexible bookkeeping job. But no matter how much she cherished being with her child all day, it was equally necessary to set a good example for her daughter. Mia's career was important. It changed lives. The work she was trained to do, the work she enjoyed, was more than a means of income. It was what she was good at…what she contributed to the world at large.

Once the résumé was polished, she compiled a list of all the influential contacts she knew in her field and emailed them her portfolio. After she clicked the send button, she felt her heart sink. She wished she had time to follow up on her attraction to Dylan. But if he was not interested, then the sooner she left, the better. Besides, getting involved with him would only lead to heartbreak. Dylan belonged in Silver Glen. Sadly, there was nothing here for Mia.

That night, Cora did not sleep well at all. She was restless and cranky, perhaps picking up on her mother's unsettled feelings. At two in the morning, Mia wandered to the other side of the house to get a glass of milk. Cora whimpered and squirmed in her arms, her little face red and blotchy from crying.

Mia knew how she felt. For two cents, she would plop down on the floor and bawl herself.

Instead of reaching for the light switch—because she definitely wanted Cora to know it was not morning—she tiptoed carefully across the kitchen, hoping to avoid a stubbed toe. But when she did run into something, it was big and warm and solid. Her muffled shriek came seconds before the realization that Dylan held her by the arms.

Her pulse racing like a train bound for the station, she wriggled free. "You've got to stop doing that. My heart can't take it." The complaint didn't hold much heat, since she was whispering.

He ran a hand over Cora's downy head. "You think she's getting a tooth?"

Mia yawned, not even protesting when Dylan reached for Cora. "It's a little too soon for that. Maybe I'm being punished for something."

"You want some company while she's awake?" His question was quiet, but it seemed significant somehow.

"I haven't seen you for days."

"Did you miss me?" Even in the gloom she could see the flash of white teeth.

"Barely noticed you were gone," she lied. "And yes…if you have insomnia, I'd love to have an adult to converse with. My repertoire of baby talk is all panned out."

Dylan brushed past her. "Follow me."

In the living room, he flipped on the gas logs, even though it was the height of summer. The dancing flames cast a rosy glow of illumination that was gentle enough not to stimulate Cora.

Mia collapsed onto the sofa, so tired she could barely sit up straight. "I can hold her," she said.

"Relax, Mia. I've got this."

As she watched through heavy-lidded eyes, Dylan walked Cora around the room, singing to her in a voice that was pleasant but definitely off-key. His husky serenade seeped into Mia's bones and muscles, relaxing them until she slid further down into the cushions.

Only then did it dawn on her that he was naked from the waist up. In the illumination from the fire, she could see the beautiful delineation of his muscles. He looked powerfully masculine, and—in spite of the baby cradled in his arms—untamed, pagan. His drawstring pajama pants, navy with a yellow stripe, were most likely a concession to his houseguests.

Cora quieted finally, lashes settling on rounded cheeks. Mia knew she should get up and take the baby, but she couldn't seem to move....

Dylan cuddled Cora. Sweet, snuggly, pudgy Cora. She rested against his chest trustingly, a little streak of drool wetting his skin. He loved babies, always had. They smelled like home and happiness and love. An infant's smile was the greatest promise that the world would go on, no matter how much the grown-ups mucked around with it. When he was sure she was out for the count, he laid her in the crib, crossing his fingers that she would stay asleep.

When she didn't stir after a full minute, he was fairly certain she was down for the night. Returning to the living room, he found Mia fast asleep, as well. She had tugged an afghan from the back of the sofa. All he could see of her was the top of her head. Smiling wryly, he bent and scooped her into his arms.

If Cora reminded him of peace and security, Mia's warm body had just the opposite effect. The weight of her in his arms gave him a jolt of excitement and possessive hunger. Holding her, he wanted to believe that it was possible to keep her here. Silver Glen was his home. If he tried hard enough, he could envision Mia returning to her roots as well.

Although he had worked hard to create himself in the

image of a carefree, never-serious party guy, he knew in his heart that the fabric of life was more than that. It was woven of simple pleasures like holding a quiet, complicated, soft-skinned woman in your arms and wondering what it would be like to kiss her.

From happier days of his childhood, he remembered his family sitting around the table playing board games and laughing, always laughing. After Reggie's death, much of the laughter had stopped. Perhaps that was why Dylan had tried so hard to be the life of the party. He remembered those good times and yearned to recreate them.

Mia reminded him anew of what he was missing. She spoke to him at a visceral level, underscoring the value of things like hard work and loyalty and selfless giving. Seeing her with Cora made him want to be a better man.

Mia's room was semidark. She had left a light on in the bathroom with the door cracked, so Dylan was able to carry her easily without crashing into furniture. With one hand he straightened the tousled sheets and spread. The state of her bed told him more than words about her interrupted night.

When he folded back the covers and laid her gently on the mattress, she stirred, her eyes opening slowly. "Cora?" She sat up on her elbows.

Dylan smoothed the hair from her face. "She's asleep. In her bed."

"Oh. I'm sorry."

"Nothing to be sorry about. There's no reason not to ask for help, Mia. As long as you're here."

"I'm making you uncomfortable. Your family has questions. And you want to draw a line in the sand between business and personal. I'll go as soon as I can find somewhere else to live."

Nine

He hadn't meant to be quite so honest.

Mia's nose wrinkled. "Ouch. Am I that much of a liability?" Though she said it jokingly, he fancied that in her eyes he saw vulnerability and hurt. But that might have been a trick of light and shadow.

He sat down beside her on the bed. "You don't belong in Silver Glen, Mia." The truth might hurt, but it was better that they each acknowledge the reality of their situation. "Your intellectual gifts can make a difference in the world. For now, you've had a hiccup. You need time to regroup. That's understandable. And I'm happy I can help. I owe you that. But we can't forget that your stay here is temporary. I've already had one relationship with a woman who was just passing through. It was a messy, public breakup. No one gets privacy in a small town. I'd rather not repeat the experience."

"That's quite a speech. Would you care to cut to the bottom line and tell me what the heck you're saying?"

"I'm saying that I want you."

He stroked her arm as he said the words, completely aware that Mia was unlike anyone he had cared about before. Beneath the very real sexual hunger he felt for her was a vein of something he couldn't pin down…tenderness maybe, but more than that. She was a part of his past, a very significant part. She had helped shape him into the man he had become.

After his blunt statement, she sat straight up, crossing her legs pretzel style and staring at him. "You may be disappointed. I'm not very good at it. Sex, I mean."

Humor slipped in unannounced, lightening the mood. "In this particular situation, I think it's safe to assume that I won't have any complaints. Not that I'm bragging, but you probably were with the wrong men before."

"Man. Only one."

"Ah, yes. The professor. I may not have his brains, but I've researched the hell out of this particular topic." Perhaps he shouldn't have alluded to other women, even obliquely. Mia was acquainted with his past exploits, but she flinched when he mentioned them.

"Are you sure, Dylan?"

Again that heartbreaking vulnerability. "We were friends once. I hope we still are. But the connection I feel to you, to the grown-up Mia, is brand-new. I'd like to see where it goes."

Only a prospective lover with Mia's IQ could induce Dylan to use such an academic approach to sex. Ordinarily, a couple of drinks, soft lighting and a willing woman took care of any negotiations in that arena. But for whatever reason, it seemed important to him that she knew he had thought about this. That he wasn't being ruled by his baser instincts.

On the other hand, his carefully worded analysis of the spark between them didn't seem to be making her very happy. Hell, why was he second-guessing everything?

Carefully, giving her one last moment to change her mind, he slid both hands beneath her sleep-ruffled hair and cupped her neck. His head lowered. Women normally closed their eyes at this point. Mia didn't. She watched him with fascination in her dark-eyed gaze.

He hesitated. "You make me a little nuts," he confessed.

"Why?" This close he could see how thick her lashes were.

"I sometimes feel like you're studying me."

"Why on earth would I do that?" Sexual anticipation was replaced by frustration on her face and in her voice.

"You're the only genius I've ever met. I don't know what goes on inside your head." Why he was baring his soul like this, he hadn't a clue. But it obviously was the wrong tack to take with Mia.

Her chin wobbled. "I'm no different than any other woman, Dylan. Same body parts, same emotions, same wants and needs. I hate it when you say things like that."

"I'm sorry." And he was.

"Forget all that other stuff. Pretend you picked me up at a bar. Not the Silver Dollar. Someplace else. We met and flirted and all we could think about was jumping each other's bones."

In that moment, he understood what she wanted. Mia needed to feel like an ordinary woman. She wasn't ordinary. Far from it. But he was hurting her by hiding the depth of his hunger, when all he had ever wanted to do was protect her.

Deliberately, he reached for the hem of her tank top and peeled it upward, forcing her to raise her arms as he lifted it over her head. His sharp, audible intake of breath was loud in the hushed silence of her room. "God, you're beautiful," he muttered. White-skinned and pleasingly curved, she was a sculptor's dream. But unlike marble, she was real and soft and warm. Locking his gaze with hers, he cupped her breasts with his hands, testing their weight and fullness.

This time Mia closed her eyes.

He took that as a positive sign. Suddenly, he felt like a kid in a candy shop, not sure what he wanted first. A lin-

ear approach seemed feasible. He started with her delicate
eyelids, drifted down her perfect nose, and settled his lips
over hers. The contact rocked him on his ass. Nuclear fis-
sion couldn't have been any hotter.

Even as his hands kneaded her flesh and teased her
nipples, his mouth ravaged hers. Tongues tangling. Breath
laboring. She was as eager as he was, her slim arms going
around his neck and tightening as he deepened the kiss. It
wasn't what he expected at all.

He had thought Mia might be tentative or clumsy or
awkward. Instead, he—Dylan—felt completely out of his
depth. She was intensely female despite the fact that she
did little to enhance her looks with the usual feminine
paints and potions. He had barely touched her, and already he was hard enough to make his position on the
bed uncomfortable.

"Mia?" he asked hoarsely, not really sure what he
wanted her to say or do.

"Take off your clothes, Dylan. Come to bed with me."

Mia couldn't believe it was really happening. All the
fantasies about Dylan she had entertained over the years
were pale imitations of the real thing. His skin was hot
beneath her touch, though the room was plenty cool. The
muscles that rippled in his arms and torso were strong and
defined. She stroked him with giddy delight. He was hers.
Maybe only for tonight. But he was hers.

Her confidence wavered when she saw him fully nude.
Standing beside the bed, arms crossed, shoulders squared,
he projected determination and an unmistakable intent to
have his way. His erection bobbed high and strong against
his flat, corded abdomen.

She swallowed against the sudden lump in her throat.
"You're a very striking man," she said quietly.

He tugged her toward the edge of the bed and dragged

her sleep pants down her legs, along with her undies. She was a grown woman. Not without experience. But allowing Dylan to look his fill of her naked body required a surprising amount of courage. Her belly was no longer as flat as it once was, and she had a couple of stretch marks.

In her imagination, this was the moment when he joined her beneath the covers. The reassuringly *covering* covers. But he took her off guard again. Gently, he took both of her hands in his, gripped them, and pulled her to her feet. She was not a noticeably short woman. But toe-to-toe with Dylan she felt small and defenseless.

His devilish grin warmed the cold places in her body. "Touch me, Mia. Please."

It reassured her to realize that his need was every bit as great as hers. She went up on tiptoe and kissed his mouth, lingering to slide her tongue between his teeth, relishing the response that quaked through his frame. Against her belly, his eager flesh twitched. She clasped him in one hand, squeezing gently. His clenched jaw and damp forehead revealed the extent of her power. Power she had never claimed before.

Tilting back her head, she searched his gaze. "Is that what you meant?"

"Damn, woman. I thought you said you weren't good at this."

She rested her cheek against his chest, feeling the steady thump of his heart. When her arms clasped his waist and his circled hers, she felt as if something precious had been born. "These are just the preliminaries," she whispered. "Don't get too excited, Dylan. I may not measure up in the main event."

She'd spent most of her life being judged on her abilities. Here, now, on the verge of having sex with the man of her dreams, it had never mattered more that she did and said the right things. It would be crushing if Dylan found her naiveté boring or, even worse, amusing.

But he totally disarmed her by laughing. "Good Lord, Mia. It isn't an exam. And besides, I'm supposed to be the one pleasing *you* tonight, not the other way around. You'll get your turn. Relax, sweetheart."

He scooped her into his arms and sprawled on the bed with her, his big, hairy legs tangling with her smaller, paler ones. Though he kept most of his weight on his hands, she shivered at the delicious feel of his tough, honed body pressing hers into the mattress. Such a primitive response. But entirely inescapable.

Scraping her thumbnail along his chin, she smiled. "I like you all rough and scraggly."

Nuzzling her neck, he chuckled. "You may sing another tune when you wake up in the morning wearing my marks. If I'd known this was a possibility, I'd have shaved for you."

She cocked her head, staring up at him. "Do things usually start off this slowly? Not that I'm complaining."

"Well, Miss Impatient, do you have condoms?"

"Um, no…" She flushed from her throat to her hairline. Just when she thought she was giving a great performance as a woman of the world having casual sex with a hot, hungry guy, she betrayed her true colors.

Though a pained look crossed his face, he spoke gently. "I'll go get some." Climbing off the bed, he towered over her. "You won't change your mind?"

She pulled the sheet over her nudity, not quite as nonchalant as she hoped to be in this situation. "I won't change my mind."

Dylan must have dabbled in time travel, because he made it to his bedroom and back to hers in a nanosecond.

After dropping a handful of packets on the bedside table, he held one out to her. "You want to do the honors?"

"No. Thank you." To be honest, she wasn't at all sure that little piece of latex was going to fit over and around Dylan's aroused shaft.

Nevertheless, he rolled it on with an economy of motion she admired and then climbed back in bed. "Move over, woman."

"Your feet are freezing," she exclaimed.

"Then warm me up."

After that, any conversation gave way to sheer physical sensation. Despite his chilled feet, the rest of Dylan's body radiated heat. He settled between her thighs with a groan that sounded as if he had waited a hundred years to find that exact spot. She wrapped her legs around his waist, lifting her hips to urge him on.

And yet still, he didn't join their bodies. His erection, hot and firm, rubbed lazily against the cleft between her legs. Zings of sensation flooded her pelvis with restless pleasure. She had known that sex with Dylan would be incredible. Sheer physical delight. What she hadn't expected was the rush of emotion. Tears stung her eyes, though she wouldn't let them fall for fear he would misunderstand.

He was so dear, so special, so deserving of a woman's love. It was incomprehensible to her that his fiancée had walked away from him. Perhaps one day the woman would realize what she had lost. Or perhaps she and Dylan were never really right for each other at all.

The girl Mia had been in high school still lived somewhere deep inside the adult Mia. That shy, backward teenager who had adored the angry, sullen Dylan now wanted the stronger, happier Dylan with equal measure. He'd thrown up barriers between them already. Telling her she didn't belong. Making his learning challenges and her intellectual capabilities some kind of überforbidden matchup.

They weren't the Montagues and Capulets.

When he braced himself on one hand and stroked his fingers over her lower lip, she tasted him involuntarily, her tongue wetting the pad of his thumb. He shuddered. She bit the same spot with a sharp nip.

Clearly Dylan had himself on a tight leash. She was well aware that he was holding back. But she didn't want his gentleness, at least not right now. Hunger rose like an irrepressible tide, making her reckless.

"I won't break," she muttered. "I want you in me, over me, on me."

His pupils expanded as hot color flushed his cheekbones. He dropped his forehead to hers. "You've got it, Mia." The words were guttural, a hoarse accompaniment to the forceful thrust of his hips that buried him deep inside her.

She was fairly certain they both gasped in unison, but with the sound of her heartbeat loud in her ears, she couldn't be sure.

Mia had the ability to convert complicated numerical equations into their metric equivalents without using a calculator. Her papers had been published in academic journals and had even been presented at international conferences. Abstract ideas and three-dimensional thinking were her bread and butter.

But what she couldn't fathom was how one man, *this* one man, could reduce her from a practical, down-to-earth scientist and mom to a shivering mass of nerves and need. She swallowed hard and tried to force words from a dry throat. "That's more like it."

Dylan nibbled her collarbone, his lower body momentarily still. His pause gave her a chance to absorb the effects of his possession. Pleasantly stretched and undeniably filled, her sex welcomed him enthusiastically, little muscle flutters massaging his length.

The hair on his chest tickled her breasts. She liked the sensation. Their coupling had an earthy, elemental rightness to it that she and the professor had never quite attained. This breathless moment seemed preordained, as if long ago, Dylan and Mia's teenage friendship prepared the ground for what was to come.

He moved his hips without warning, gaining another half inch of penetration. "You're tight," he groaned. "I don't want this to end."

"You've barely started yet," she pointed out, a little miffed that her charms weren't sufficient enough to drive him insane with lust.

Dylan didn't answer with words. Instead, he began moving slowly, drawing a tremulous cry from her parched throat. Beneath her, his expensive sheets were cool and smooth against her heated flesh. Above her, his big, hard body enveloped her in a stimulating mélange of sight and sound and touch. The room smelled of warm skin and hot sex.

"Open your mouth, baby."

When she obeyed, the thrust of his tongue mimicked the movements of his hips. The dual possession melted her, incinerated her. Feverish and desperate, she raked his shoulders with her fingernails, barely conscious that she did so. "Please," she whispered. "Please."

Impossible pleasure beckoned, her orgasm building with the heat of a thousand suns, barely contained. Dylan took her again and again, his movements bold, giving no quarter. She would be sore tomorrow. That fleeting thought escaped from some last coherent corner of her brain.

"Come for me, Mia," he rasped, the words barely audible.

And she did.…

Dylan held her as she writhed and cried out. He ground the base of his erection against her mound, sending her up yet again. Feeling her climax, watching the sharp jolt of completion paint her face with rosy color, sent exultation fizzing in his veins, despite the fact that he had thus far denied himself release.

Holding back was next to impossible, but he wanted to enjoy her pleasure. When she was sated and still, her eyes closed, he withdrew and leaned down to whisper in her ear. "You screamed my name," he said smugly.

Mia opened one eyelid. "Did not."

"Did, too."

Playing with her was fun. But fun was not even on the scale of what he needed now. "I'll let you sleep soon," he promised, not at all sure he wasn't lying. He rolled to his back, taking her limp body with him. Arranging her like a sleepy rag doll with her legs straddling his hips, he lifted her gently, positioned the head of his erection at her entrance and pushed.

Mia's lips parted, an arrested expression on her face. "Oh," she breathed, her hands settling on his shoulders.

Oh, indeed. The new angle put increasing pressure on his hypersensitive sex. Straining to give her as much as she could take, he flexed his hips and drove upward, shaking the bed with the force of his rhythmic movements. Mia's hair fell around her face. Her breasts swung enticingly above him.

Rearing up, he captured one nipple with his teeth and sucked it into his mouth. Mia moaned. He felt the clasp of her inner flesh tighten around him. The visual stimulation and the feel of her in his arms snapped the last of his control. He rolled the two of them again, needing the mattress to brace against as he lunged wildly toward the finish.

Holy hell. Sharp yellow lights obscured his vision. Uncontrollable trembling sapped his muscles of their strength. Lightning struck his groin with paralyzing heat, and he slammed into the end with a shout.

Ten

Dylan lay stunned on top of Mia, barely able to breathe. What in the hell had happened to him? Instinctively, he gathered his defenses, unwilling to let her see that their lovemaking was anything out of the ordinary. Already, Mia knew far too much about his psyche for him to feel completely at ease with her. A man liked to hide his weaknesses.

It remained to be seen, however, if the last hour was a weakness or a catastrophic shift in the continental plates.

When he thought he could force his muscles to move, he lifted away from her, stumbled to his feet and went into the bathroom to take care of the condom and splash water on his face. In the mirror his eyes were overbright, feverish. He ran both hands through his hair, raking his fingers across his scalp.

When he returned to the bedroom, braced for the inevitable postcoital conversation, Mia was sound asleep. She lay on her back where he had abandoned her, arms outflung, hair mussed, her body bare as the day she was born. He couldn't decide if relief or disappointment held the upper hand. Looking at her made his chest hurt and his head throb.

What had he done?

The clock ticked away the minutes before dawn. Mia needed her sleep. Even if he was already partially erect and wanted her again with an alarming desperation, it would be cruel to wake her. Cora was a lively handful. A rested Mia would be better able to handle her daughter's demands.

Quietly picking up his scattered pieces of clothing, he bundled them into his arms and lingered by the bed. Mia and his ex-fiancée, Tara, were as different as two women could be—in looks, in temperament, in every way. What did it say about him that he had so quickly recovered from a broken heart? Had Tara's defection been more a blow to his pride?

In all honesty, the sex with Tara had been fun. And she had been fun. Always urging him on to the next wild adventure. In retrospect, it was kind of ironic. Tara was a female version of himself, or at least the self he had been in high school and later as a young adult.

Maybe that had been the attraction. He understood her.

Mia, on the other hand, was a complete mystery. Even given her history of crippling shyness, it was hard to imagine that no man had managed to put a ring on her finger. She was warm and funny and loyal and brave. That she had resorted to a sperm donor to become pregnant baffled him.

Such an action pointed to the fact that she didn't want any messy involvement with a man who might make demands. Had she never been in love? Ever?

Now that he thought about it, he surely hadn't. The relationship with Tara had been two parts lust and one part male hubris. Dating a beautiful actress made him feel like a million bucks. He could be excused for believing their short-lived engagement was the real thing, because he'd been thinking with his male anatomy and not his brain.

He liked to imagine that in the intervening years he had matured. At least he'd been smart enough not to get entwined in any further unsuitable relationships. His dating nowadays was light and fun. No commitment, no complications.

Up until tonight.

He backed away from the bed a step at a time, his feet silent on the plush carpet. When he reached the door, he opened it quietly. Mia slept so deeply, she never even stirred.

The bed and the woman were inviting. All he had to do was lift the covers and take her in his arms. His hands tingled as he imagined the feel of her skin. Warm. Incredibly soft.

Damn. He had a sick feeling that he had let the genie out of the bottle. What was he going to do about Mia and Cora now?

Mia rolled over and glanced at her phone to see what time it was. Weak, early-morning sunlight filtered into the room through a crack in the heavy brocade drapes that matched the moss-green color palette of the room. Her breasts ached, heavy with milk. Cora would be awake any moment now. On the monitor, the grainy picture of Mia's daughter showed a reassuring image of the infant sleeping peacefully.

Concentrating on the baby wasn't working. Movielike flashes spun through Mia's head. Arousing, incredible memories. She needed to believe that the stimulating pictures were nothing more than a surreal dream. But the fragrance of a man's skin lingered on her sheets.

Even as her legs moved restlessly, her heart and soul ached with the breath-stealing certainty that she and Dylan had been lovers last night. In the wee hours when rational thought was easily subverted by yearning and need. During the drowsy moments when phantoms seemed real and the concrete world faded into shadows.

The emptiness of the bed mocked her. If the dreams were real, where was Dylan? Why wasn't he curled up with her beneath the sumptuous covers, his body warm and hard and ready for a morning tête-à-tête?

Shaking all over, she fled to the bathroom, taking the baby monitor with her. If she were lucky, she would have time for a quick shower before Cora demanded her breakfast. Beneath the hot, pelting spray, Mia soaped herself furiously, trying to erase the feel of Dylan's touch.

His absence spoke volumes. Even in the beginning, he had expressed his doubts. Perhaps he had been looking to her to put a stop to the madness that had caught them up in the middle of the night.

Mia hadn't been interested in making rational, grown-up decisions. Dylan had stood before her, wanting her. So she took without asking, without considering Cora, without deciding if her selfish behavior had consequences. What did Dylan think of her? Why wasn't he here?

Closing her heart to the pain she didn't want to face, she returned to the bedroom to dress. By the time she had finished, Cora was stirring. As she went to scoop up her daughter and change her diaper, Mia reminded herself how lucky she was. Cora was the sunshine in her life. The one true lodestar that kept her focused and reminded her that a mother's job was to be selfless…to put her child's well-being ahead of her own.

Mia was in Silver Glen so Cora would have a roof overhead while her mother found a job. Touching base with Dylan had accomplished that. He needed Mia's help, and she heeded his. But their bargain had a definite timeline. A beginning and an end.

As she sat in the rocking chair nursing her daughter, the familiarity of the routine brought some peace to her heart. Dylan wasn't hers. She'd known that at fifteen and she knew it now. Her only mistake had been thinking sex with him would end the wondering and the wanting.

Well, now she knew. Sex with Dylan was deserving of

all the superlatives she could summon. But she wouldn't embarrass him by letting him think she was expecting more. Neither more intimacy nor more attention. She was living in his house because of a fluke. It would be wrong to put him in an awkward position by burdening him with her feelings.

When Cora was finished, Mia dressed her in a teal-and-yellow sundress. Mia's stomach was growling so loudly she knew it was impractical to put off breakfast any longer. As she suspected, when she and Cora entered the kitchen, there was no sign of Dylan. Only Gertie…frying bacon.

The older woman turned and smiled. "There you two are. I had a feeling someone kept you up during the night, Mia."

Mia felt her cheeks redden and hoped the housekeeper didn't notice. "Yes, as usual. I came in here for a glass of milk, but thankfully Cora finally settled down and slept until morning."

Without asking, Gertie waved Mia to a seat and put a bowl of fresh strawberries and blueberries in front of her. "I've got some cinnamon muffins coming out of the oven in about a minute. Eat up."

"Did Dylan have an early appointment?"

"Not to my knowledge. He left about thirty minutes ago to head down to the Silver Dollar. Why? Did you need to speak to him?"

"I did have a few questions about the books. But it can wait."

Mia had barely finished her meal when the landline phone rang. Gertie answered it and then held out the cordless receiver to Mia. "It's for you. Ms. Kavanagh."

Gertie swooped in and scooped Cora from Mia's lap. Mia answered reluctantly. "Hello?"

"Good morning, Mia. This is Maeve. Zoe and I have put our heads together, and we would like for you and Dylan to come to dinner tonight up at the lodge. Zoe wants to cook for us. We have several portable cribs here for the hotel guests. We can set one up in Zoe and Liam's bedroom, so you can put Cora to sleep and not have to rush off."

"But, Ms. Kavanagh, I have no idea if Dylan is available."

"Call me Maeve. Please. I've already talked to him this morning. He said it was up to you."

Mia was stuck. Social convention dictated that she accept the invitation, but she could think of nothing more awkward than sitting across the dinner table from the mother of the man with whom she'd been naked the night before. Since she didn't have a valid reason to decline, however, she was forced to agree. "Well, yes, then. That would be lovely. And thank you for making arrangements for Cora. Since I'm nursing, I don't want to be away from her for too long."

"I understand completely. We'll look forward to seeing the three of you around six-thirty. Oh, and Mia?"

"Yes?"

"Would it be a problem to dress for dinner? Zoe has worked hard on this meal, and I thought it would be fun to celebrate."

"Not a problem at all. See you soon."

Mia hung up the phone wondering ruefully when she had become such a good liar. Dress for dinner? Good grief. She had brought all of her clothes with her to Silver Glen except for winter things that were in storage, but she had no idea if she could find anything suitable, since most of the cartons were still out in the garage.

When she asked Gertie to help with the baby so Mia could rummage in her boxes, Gertie offered a solution. "After the baby's next feeding, why don't you put her down for a nap and let me keep an eye on her? You could go into town and visit that cute little shop called Silver Linings.

They have beautiful things for women your age. I'm sure you can find what you want."

"I hate to take up your time, Gertie."

The woman, still holding Cora, waved a hand dismissively. "If I have to choose between babysitting or doing the laundry, it's no competition. Go. Have a few hours to yourself. All new moms need that. I swear I'll take good care of her."

"I know you will."

Mia's other problem wasn't so easily solved. It seemed self-indulgent in the extreme to buy a new dress for herself when her finances were so tight. On the other hand, wearing the appropriate feminine armor for the night to come would go a long way toward helping her face Dylan.

She needed something that would make it clear, without words, that she knew the score and was confident in her own skin. A sexy frock that would knock his socks off and at the same time convince him she had no designs on his bachelorhood.

By the time Cora fell asleep right after lunch, Mia was itching to get out of the house. She hadn't realized how much she had been *chained* to Cora's side until she had the opportunity to be out and about without a diaper bag or a stroller. Not that she was unhappy with her new role. She loved being Cora's mom. Every minute of it.

Still, the prospect of stealing away for a couple of carefree hours held definite appeal.

Gertie's directions were spot on. Silver Linings had not been around when Mia was a girl. The trendy shop occupied the ground floor of a historic building adjacent to the bank. When Mia parked and got out to glance in the storefront windows, a little flutter of excitement skittered down her spine. There, on a mannequin, was the exact dress she'd imagined.

Nursing moms were often limited in their choice of

clothing due to necessity, but this dress opened down the front. Without wasting further time, she went inside to try it on.

The salesclerk was a young woman several years younger than Mia. "I'm Dottie. May I help you find something?" she asked politely. Her nose was pierced and she had a tattoo down her left forearm. In high school, this was the sort of person who'd looked down at Mia and made fun of her. But Mia was an adult now and no longer cowed by the idea of someone judging her. It had been a long road, but she was happy with who she was.

"The red dress in the window? May I try it on? I became a mom not that long ago, and my wardrobe is in need of help." Fortunately, the store had her size. Otherwise she would have had to swallow her disappointment and choose something else. Though she took three additional dresses into the changing room, she had her heart set on the sexy one from the window display.

Stripping down to her bra and panties, she stepped into the sleeveless, cocktail-length dress. It was not at all conventional. The fabric was a heavy watered silk. The design featured a nipped-in waist and a skirt that flared slightly in a bell shape. The back was scooped out, but the front dipped into a low V topped with a single pea-size clear crystal that served as the zipper pull.

Even before she zipped up the dress, Mia knew her bra would have to go. Unfastening the undergarment and dropping it onto a stool, she stared at her bare breasts in the mirror, reminded of the hungry way Dylan had gazed at her. And then touched her....

Her nipples ached as they furled tightly. She would have liked to blame the telling response on the air-conditioning, but the small space was actually quite warm.

As Mia struggled to close the bodice, the saleslady

spoke from just outside the door. "How are you doing in there?"

Mia grimaced at her reflection. "This is the same size I always wear, but…"

The clerk's voice was sympathetic. "Don't worry if you still have a few pounds of baby weight to lose. It will come off in no time. Do you need me to bring you another size?"

"It's not that. Look at me." She opened the door. "Tell me what you think."

The young woman's eyes widened and she grinned. "Ah. Now I get it. You've got nursing boobs. I say enjoy them while they last. Same thing happened to me when my son was born. My husband loved it."

Mia's cheeks warmed. The woman in the mirror had Mia's face and hair, but beyond that she seemed like a stranger. The bombshell image made her uncomfortable. She'd spent most of her life trying to blend into the wood-work. This dress made a statement, even more so because of her breasts. "You don't think there's too much…"

"Cleavage?"

"Yes."

"Not at all. You're probably not used to showing off your body. I see it all the time. Just because you've got a kid doesn't mean you have to wear a shroud. You've got a kickin' figure. And if I'm not mistaken, you're hoping to catch someone's eye with this—right?"

"It's a small dinner party."

"You didn't answer my question. Which is as good as a yes. Buy the dress. You know you want to." She glanced at the three hanging on a hook at Mia's shoulder. Turning up her nose, she shook her head. "Those other ones are fine if you're presenting an award to the parent-teacher association or visiting your grandma's church. But if you want to say, 'I'm available,' then the red is your best bet."

Mia swallowed her misgivings. "I'll take it."

Three hours later she had a mild panic attack. If it had been feasible, she would have ripped open every one of her moving boxes until she found a nice, safe, boring outfit to wear tonight. But it was about a thousand degrees out in the hot, muggy garage, and besides, Dylan was going to be ready to leave in less than half an hour.

She still hadn't seen or heard from him today. Not so much as a peep, other than a terse text indicating their time of departure. Clearly, he had chatted with his mother and knew the plan.

Once more, Mia looked in the ornate, full-length mirror. Her strappy black sandals were not new, but they were comfy and flattering. She had left her hair loose and wavy on her shoulders. For once, the style was cooperating, though all bets were off when she had to step outside into the heat and humidity.

But between her head and her toes, there was a revolution going on. Somehow, the new dress looked even more outrageous than it had in the store dressing room. The fit was perfect at the waist. The hemline was elegant, flattering her legs. But the top? Holy cow. She looked like a Victoria's Secret model. Breasts that had never been more than a B cup now thrust up and out in all their rounded glory.

How had she not noticed before? On maternity leave, her clothing of choice had been T-shirts, nursing bras and sweatpants. Her biggest goal during the first six weeks had been not to burst into tears more than once a day. With her hormones all over the map, she had felt frumpy, overwhelmed and inexperienced.

Noticing that her breasts had morphed from barely there to bountiful hadn't been on her radar.

Tucking her hair behind her ear, she made one last pirouette and put a hand to her fluttery stomach. For better or for worse, it was showtime.

Eleven

Dylan ran a finger inside his collar, trying to loosen his tie without removing it and starting all over again. What had his mother and Zoe been thinking? He hated wearing a tux. The more formal dress reminded him that he was a Kavanagh and thus on display to the community all the time. Dylan didn't want to be *anyone's* role model.

He much preferred the comfort of his jeans and cowboy boots. In his role at the Silver Dollar, he could pretend he was like all the rest of the working stiffs. But tonight, dressed in an expensive European-made jacket and trousers that he wore as seldom as possible, he felt as if he were playing a part. Liam wore dress clothes effortlessly. In fact, Dylan sometimes wondered if his older brother had his boxers starched and pressed.

It was no picnic following along in school behind the sibling who excelled at everything. Liam's academic awards and accolades had taken over his bedroom bookshelves by the time he was sixteen, along with an equal number of sporting trophies.

Dylan had his own ribbons and medals and letterman jackets, but he would have traded it all for just one visible, pen-on-paper acknowledgement that he had a decent brain.

Shaking off the stupid childhood trauma of never measuring up, he pulled the car around front, turned on the AC and moved Cora's infant seat from Mia's vehicle to his. Since they were both going to be dressed to the nines, he wanted to pamper his date in something other than his utilitarian, though expensive, pickup truck. The late model Mercedes had been a gift from his mother, a reminder that he was one of the family no matter how hard he tried to pretend otherwise.

The Kavanagh wealth made him uncomfortable. Especially since he was the only one in the family with no discernible talent or passion. He didn't *excel* at anything.

As he walked back through the front door into the house, he stopped dead in his tracks. Mia had just stepped into the living room. When she saw him, she halted as well. "Hello, Dylan." Her voice was polite…cool…no inflection at all.

Despite her somewhat chilly greeting, his temperature shot through the roof and his mouth dried like a snowflake in Death Valley. The woman standing in front of him was no longer merely an attractive female with whom he'd had sex. She was a goddess…or an angel. He couldn't decide which. Dark, shiny hair tumbled artfully onto white shoulders. Deft, completely natural-looking makeup accentuated her eyes, making them bittersweet chocolate instead of the lighter, milkier variety.

Dangling earrings fabricated of some clear, faceted material caught the light, drawing attention to her swanlike neck. Her lips were red. Sin-red. A shade to match her dress and make a man shudder with desire.

But it was the single glittery bead at the top of her bodice that caught his attention. The small piece of glass was attached to a zipper that ran the entire length of the dress. All a man would have to do is tug gently, but inexorably, and in seconds the woman would be naked.

He cleared his throat. "You look very nice."

A small frown creased the space between her eyebrows. "So do you."

Gertie, toting the baby on her hip, came in from the kitchen at that moment, rescuing Dylan and Mia from their awkward conversation. She whistled. "Lord, have mercy. You two clean up real nice. See, Cora. Look how pretty your mama is. And my boy, Dylan. Why, if I was forty years younger, I'd take a run at him myself."

Dylan kissed Gertie's cheek and the top of Cora's head. "You're good for my ego, but don't go overboard. You know you'll always be my favorite." He took the baby, who immediately tried to grab for his bow tie. "You ready, Mia?"

She nodded. "Yes."

Her stilted response pretty much set the tone for their drive up the mountain. The Silver Beeches Lodge, constructed after the Second World War, was an elegant and outrageously expensive hotel that catered to high-end clients who demanded privacy and discretion. From the silver screen to politics, the majority of guests had money and wielded power.

As they drove up onto a sweeping flagstone apron, Dylan shot a sideways glance at his passenger. She sat primly, knees pressed together, hands clasped on the small black clutch purse in her lap. Cora had babbled happily during the short trip, diverted by the sights and sounds outside the car.

As the valet approached, Dylan drummed his fingers on the steering wheel. "Shouldn't we get our stories straight?" he asked.

For the first time, Mia looked straight at him, her gaze stormy. "I don't think we have a story. So no problem."

"You're mad because I wasn't there when you woke up." He still felt bad about that. But he'd had to get out of the house, had needed physical distance to clear his head and analyze what had happened to him when he made love to Mia. If he'd had his way, he would have avoided her even longer, but tonight's dinner was in the nature of a command performance.

Mia's eyes narrowed. "I'm not mad. Not at all. Sleep is far sweeter than anything else I could be doing these days."

Wow. Direct hit. She'd just relegated mind-blowing sex to a spot somewhere below snoozing. Fair enough. If that's how she wanted to play it... Opening his car door with a jerk that nearly twisted it off the hinges, he went to the back and talked to Cora while he released her from her seat. The baby's smile took the sharp edges off his anger.

In his peripheral vision, he saw Mia get out of the car and smooth her skirt. Five men stood on the steps of the hotel, some guests, some employees. Five sets of eyes locked on Mia and stared. He couldn't blame them. She radiated sexuality. Her lush breasts were evidence of the elemental, primitive truth that mankind needed a fertile woman for the continuation of the species.

Except for the occasional moment of temptation, Dylan had little interest in fathering children. But Neanderthal or not, he understood the urge to mate. Only in his case, the urge was surprisingly more than physical. He was proud of Mia, not for her breasts or her killer legs, but for her incredible brain that had so much to offer society. And for other equally important things like her care with Cora, and her gentle acceptance of a high-school boy who had done his best to alienate her.

Even if she *was* pissed at him, he was glad they were friends. Although after last night, the *friend* word could be called into question. She certainly deserved to be angry. Walking out on her after sex had been unconscionable, despite the fact he *had* needed to retreat and figure out what was going on inside his head.

In spite of all his reservations, he liked the family tableau they made. Mia insisted on taking the baby as they ascended the shallow steps. "I'll carry her."

He surrendered without protest, guessing that the baby acted as a sort of shield. It had to be intimidating for Mia to walk into the Silver Beeches knowing that she was going to be sharing dinner with Maeve Kavanagh. His mother came by her reputation honestly. She was kind and fair, but he'd seen big strong men quake in their boots when she was displeased about something.

"Liam and Zoe have an apartment on the top floor," he said. The elevator ride was silent, save for Cora's little baby sounds. She enjoyed playing with her reflection in the mirror. Fortunately, she was too young to comprehend that the adults momentarily caged in the small space were not speaking. Or to notice that their body language was hostile.

When they exited the elevator, Dylan took Mia's elbow and steered her to the right. Liam answered the doorbell on the first ring. The eldest Kavanagh son greeted them warmly. "Zoe's been on pins and needles. It's about time you got here."

Dylan curled an arm around Mia's waist, surprising her. "This is Mia. Mia, Liam."

Liam shook Mia's hand, but his attention was on Cora. "May I?" he asked. At Mia's bemused nod, he reached for the baby and called out over his shoulder. "Zoe. Come see what I found, my love."

Zoe Kavanagh was bright and beautiful and artlessly charming. The gold lace camisole and flirty skirt she wore along with gold, high-heeled pumps suited her airy personality. Even without the bright clothing, she would have lit up the room. Mia envied her easy social skills. The slender blonde rarely sat still, scooting back and forth from the kitchen to grab something or the other. "It's almost ready," she said.

Liam's smile as he watched his wife was telling. He

was deeply in love and not afraid to show it. "My Zoe insists on cooking for me even though we have a five-star chef presiding over the restaurant downstairs. But I have to admit she's a natural. I'm sure I've gained five pounds or more since we got married."

Given that Liam was as lean and toned and muscular as his brother, Mia wondered if he were joking. She had refused a glass of wine and was sipping tonic water when the door of the apartment burst open after a brief knock and Maeve Kavanagh sailed into the room followed by a handsome man who bore a striking resemblance to the two male Kavanaghs already present.

"Look who I brought with me," Maeve beamed. "I convinced Aidan to fly down for the evening." Maeve's plum Jackie-O sheath was accessorized with a matching short-sleeved jacket.

After a flurry of introductions all around, and lots of hugging, Mia found herself shaking hands with Aidan, who was as tall as his brothers, but even more suave and polished than Liam. "I feel like I'm intruding," she said, shooting a sharp, disapproving glance at Dylan.

Aidan kissed the back of her hand with a gesture that seemed completely natural. "Not at all. I'm the party crasher. I live in New York, but you'll find me here in Silver Glen frequently. Despite being a city dweller now, I can't resist the lure of home. I was hoping the whole gang would show up here tonight."

Zoe wrinkled her nose. "Conor, Patrick, Gavin and James all *claimed* to be otherwise occupied."

Liam put an arm around his wife's waist. "It's hard to corral everyone on short notice. But we'll try again soon."

Maeve threw up her hands and made a beeline for Mia. "There's that precious baby."

Dylan and Liam snickered. "You know that's the only reason she came," Dylan said in a stage whisper.

As Maeve took Cora from Mia's arms, Zoe paused long enough to put her hands on her hips and pout. "Hey, I think I've been insulted."

Liam gave his wife a long, enthusiastic kiss that soothed her ruffled feathers. When they came up for air, his throat was flushed and his eyes glittered. "I'm sure she'll be just as excited, my love, when and if you give her a grandchild."

Mia was the only one standing close enough to hear his muttered comment. And she was sure it wasn't for public consumption. Zoe's cheeks turned a delightful shade of pink and her smile softened before she escaped to the kitchen.

Amidst conversation and laughter, the finishing touches were added to the table. Mia helped, since her child had been kidnapped by the force of Maeve's personality and seemed quite happy. Just before they sat down, a second knock sounded at the door.

"I'll get it," Maeve said, the baby comfortably settled on her hip. "I asked one of our summer employees to come up and entertain Cora in Liam and Zoe's den. Paula is a senior at the University of North Carolina, majoring in child development. I hope you don't mind, Mia."

What could she say? "Of course not. It will be nice to enjoy an uninterrupted meal." Honestly, she was being spoiled. After all the help from Gertie and Dylan's family, it might be a challenge to manage on her own.

Dylan came close enough to whisper in her ear. "I'll apologize in advance for anything my mother says or does to upset you."

Mia shook her head briefly. "It's fine." She was still trying to get accustomed to Dylan's magnificence in formal attire. The snowy white shirt brought out his tan, and the traditional black tux fit his body as if it had been made for him. It probably had.

She liked the casual Dylan very much. But this sophisticated Dylan made her shiver.

As the adults seated themselves at the table, Zoe brought out the last dish and joined them. "We won't stand on ceremony," she said. "Pass the food and help yourself."

Amidst the clatter of silverware and china and crystal, Mia absorbed the atmosphere and studied the Kavanagh family. Zoe seemed a natural part of the bunch, even though she and Liam hadn't been married all that long. She laughed and shared anecdotes and teased her husband. Liam and Dylan and Aidan bickered amiably, as siblings did, covering every subject from sports to movies to politics. Maeve had strong opinions and wasn't afraid to express them.

Only Mia was silent. She wasn't *afraid* to speak. But the conversational dynamic was such that she found it difficult to get a word in edgewise. During a momentary lull in the rapid-fire back-and-forth chatter, Maeve launched her first volley, taking Mia completely off guard.

The older woman took a sip of wine, set down her glass and pinned Mia with a deceptively gentle stare. "So tell me, Mia," she said. "Is the baby's father in the picture?"

Mia choked on a piece of walnut in her salad and Dylan had to pat her on the back. Hard.

He glared at his mother. "I thought you were the woman who hated gossip."

Maeve didn't look the least bit repentant. "I do. Which is why I'm going directly to the source. But Mia can tell me to mind my own business if she wants to." She smiled at Mia. "You can, my dear, honestly."

Mia felt her face and neck turning red as the eyes of her dinner companions fixed on her with varying degrees of sympathy. "It's no secret," she said. "I was ready to have a baby, and since there was no man in my life, I chose to use a sperm donor."

Silence fell.

"I see." Maeve's perplexed expression held a hint of disapproval.

Mia was used to that by now. If she had decided as a single person to adopt an infant, no one would have batted an eye, but somehow, the path she had chosen was far less acceptable. Perhaps it was the clinical nature of the process. Or the lack of loving conception.

Zoe broke the uncomfortable impasse. "So, Mia. How did you and Dylan meet?"

Again, Mia was taken aback. She had assumed someone would have filled Zoe in before Mia and Dylan arrived, but maybe this was supposed to be a secret. Liam had been away at college when Dylan was a senior, so he and Mia had never met. But surely the family had realized Dylan was getting tutoring help. Aidan had been a sophomore or junior at the time.

Mia opened her mouth to speak, but before she could explain, Maeve rushed into the breach, addressing her daughter-in-law. "Dylan and Mia knew each other back in high school. They reconnected recently."

Zoe nodded, satisfied with that explanation. "And what do you do for a living, Mia?" she asked.

"I'm a medical researcher. But the funding for my lab and my program was cut off recently. I came back to Silver Glen for a visit and ran into Dylan at the Silver Dollar."

Dylan picked up the tale. "My bookkeeper quit, so Mia is helping me out temporarily since she's between jobs."

Zoe's eyebrows went up. "You must be very smart," she said, studying Mia's face as if she could see IQ points written there.

"Off-the-charts smart," Dylan said, his smile rueful. "I'm lucky she was available to help me out."

Mia was desperate to change the subject. As Zoe stood and began to clear the dessert plates, Mia leaped to her feet as well. "Let me help," she said. "Please. The dinner was amazing."

In the kitchen Zoe began rinsing china. "Liam tells me to let the housekeeper take care of this in the morning, but I can't stand a messy kitchen." She handed Mia a plate to put in the dishwasher. "What about you? Do you like to cook?"

"I don't really have much opportunity. I worked all the time before Cora was born, and now I'm still learning how to care for an infant. There don't seem to be enough hours in the day."

Zoe nodded, her expression thoughtful. "The Kavanaghs can be a bit overwhelming, especially when the whole clan gets together. You and I should stick together."

"I think you have the wrong idea. I work for Dylan."

"Maeve told me you're living with him."

"Only because the building burned. I was supposed to be staying in the apartment upstairs above the Silver Dollar."

Zoe rolled her eyes. "Men don't take women into their homes without some kind of ulterior motive."

He feels like he owes me something for the past.

But Mia couldn't say that. Not when Dylan's brother and sister-in-law apparently did not know how severely Dylan had struggled in high school. "Dylan is a kind man. He told me that rental property is hard to find in Silver Glen. If it had been just me, I'm sure he would have let me fend for myself. But he has a soft spot for Cora. That's probably why he suggested that she and I move in."

Zoe dried her hands on a towel and turned on the dishwasher. "Is the baby his?"

Because the other woman's back was turned, Mia couldn't see her face. "No. Of course not."

Mia's hostess faced her with a look in her eyes that told Mia she was not easily duped. "You might have concocted that story to give yourself time to figure out what to do. Not that I would blame you. The Kavanaghs would go nuts if they thought Cora was the first of the next generation. I should know. The hints have been flying thick and fast for me to get pregnant."

"Well, she's not," Mia said, the words flat. "Maybe I was naive to do what I did, but I adore Cora and I wouldn't change a thing. I know the father was healthy and normal in every way. That's enough for me."

"I didn't mean to make you angry." Zoe's big blue eyes shimmered with emotion.

Mia swallowed her pique. "I'm not angry. More defensive, I guess. I never expected people to react so strongly, my parents included."

"Do they live close by?"

"No. They're in Florida. My mom came up for the first ten days to help. She loves the baby, of course, but I could tell from the first moment I told them I was pregnant that they thought I needed a flesh-and-blood man and not an anonymous donor."

"Dylan's a man." Zoe's sly smile was not at all hard to decipher.

"Dylan and I are *not* an item."

"I watched the way he watches you. He's possessive. Though I suppose he might not even realize he feels that way. Men can be clueless about these things."

"You're way off base, Zoe. His broken engagement burned him. He's not interested in marriage or fatherhood or any commitment at all, for that matter. If you're planning on matchmaking, you should know that he and I are not a couple. Period."

Twelve

He and I are not a couple. Period.

Dylan winced, pausing just outside the kitchen door. He'd caught only the tail end of Mia's statement, but it was enough to understand the gist of her conversation with Zoe. Apparently, Dylan's sister-in-law had been understandably curious about Mia's relationship with Dylan, and Mia had set her straight.

Dylan should be elated that Mia knew the score. No need for an embarrassing face-to-face where he had to explain that he had no plans to settle down, much less with a ready-made family.

In that case, why did he feel like he'd been punched in the stomach? Striding into the kitchen, he faced the two women whose faces held identical guilty looks. "Paula says Cora is getting fussy. They're waiting for you in Zoe and Liam's bedroom. Isn't it time to feed her and put her down?" He addressed his comments to Mia impassively.

Mia, clad in the ruby dress that made her look more like a Russian princess than a new mom, glanced at the clock on the wall. "Oh, gosh, yes. Zoe and I were having so much fun getting to know each other I lost track of time."

"I'll bet you were." He wanted Mia to squirm a little, wondering whether or not he had heard what she said.

Zoe piped up, her expression beseeching. "Would you

like me to sit with you while you feed her? I assume you're nursing?"

Dylan kissed his sister-in-law's cheek. It wasn't her fault that things were weird. "I'll sit with her, Zoe. But thanks for offering. Go snuggle up with your husband on the sofa. He's looking neglected."

They exited the kitchen as a trio. Zoe headed for the living room, and Dylan and Mia searched out the master suite. As promised, the crib was set up and ready. Two comfy armchairs by the window, each with matching ottomans, offered an ideal spot for Zoe to feed Cora.

The young college student handed Cora over with a smile. "Your baby is adorable, and so even-tempered. Thank you for giving me the opportunity to play with her. The diaper bag is there on the bed. If you need baby-sitting help any other time this summer, please feel free to call me. Mrs. Kavanagh has my contact info."

Mia smiled. "Thank you, Paula. I'll keep that in mind."

When the door closed, Dylan rummaged in Cora's tote for pajamas, diapers, wipes and a changing pad to protect the bedspread. "There you go," he said, determined not to give Mia a chance to kick him out. "All set."

Mia clutched the baby. "Why are you in here? This is pretty much a solo operation."

He shrugged. "Give me the kid. Go sit in the chair and I'll bring her to you." It was a matter of minutes to change the diaper and tuck Cora into soft pajamas that snapped up the front. In his peripheral vision, he was aware that Mia had cooperated with his instructions. He was under no illusions. If she told him to leave, he would have to obey her wishes. But he was counting on the fact that she would let him stay.

When he turned and walked toward the window and the woman who stared at him with big, dark eyes, he felt something shift inside him. The setting lent a certain note of intimacy, but it was more than that.

Mia took Cora from him, her gaze unreadable. "Will you turn your back, please?"

He crouched beside her. "I'd rather not. I've seen all there is of you to see, Mia. Remember? Last night?" Slowly, giving her time to protest, he caught the crystal at the center of her bodice and began to pull.

She slapped at his hand, her cheeks hot with what appeared to be mortification. "Don't be ridiculous, Dylan. There's nothing remotely sexy about what I'm getting ready to do."

Surprisingly, a lump in his throat made it hard to speak. "That's where you're wrong." Locking her gaze with his, never looking down, he opened the zipper, hearing the soft rasp as the sides of the dress parted. In Mia's eyes he saw confusion and vulnerability and something else. Desire.

The desire was a welcome sight, because he had been wondering if it was wrong to be turned on by the prospect of Mia offering her breast to a hungry child. At last, the zipper reached the end of its track. Unable to resist any longer, he stared at the bountiful sight that was Mia's bosom. A single drop of pale milk clung to one nipple. He caught it on his finger and tasted it. "Lucky baby," he said. The words were hoarse.

Mia's lower lip trembled. What was she thinking as she stared at him so intently? As he watched, she tucked the infant in her arm and let Cora nuzzle until she found her goal and latched on. As the child sucked at her mother's breast, Dylan felt an answering pull in his groin. He shifted the second chair closer and sat down, wrapped in some mystical moment that shut out the world and enclosed Mia, Cora and him in perfect intimacy.

Mia kept her eyes downcast, her free hand coming up now and again to stroke Cora's small, perfect head. When it was time, she switched the baby to the opposite breast. Without asking, Dylan reached in his back pocket and extracted a handkerchief. Leaning forward, he carefully dried Mia's skin where the baby had eaten so enthusiastically.

He didn't linger, nor did he do anything else that might be construed as sexual. The quiet tableau was almost sacred to him. This ancient, elemental, perfectly *right* moment where life, *literally* life, was offered to the helpless in an act of love.

When Cora's long eyelashes settled on rounded cheeks, Mia pulled her away from the breast and handed her to Dylan. "Hold her please."

As he watched in silence, Mia removed the last of the sticky milk and refastened her gown. When she was fully clothed once more, she held out her arms. "I'll put her in the bed."

"Let me." He deposited Cora in the crib, smiling when she never even moved. Poor babe was tired out from an evening of fun and attention. He turned to face Mia. "Thank you."

She was still seated, her fingers moving restlessly on the arms of the chair. "For what?"

"For letting me be here. For sharing Cora. For trusting me." He pulled her to her feet. "I'm sorry I didn't stay last night."

Mia had kicked off her shoes before she fed the baby, and now, standing in front of him, she seemed fragile and helpless. Even though Dylan liked the role of protector, he knew Mia didn't need him. Not really. She was strong and smart and well able to care for herself and her offspring.

She pulled away from his grasp, her expression guarded. "Why didn't you stay?"

"Lots of reasons." *I was getting in too deep. You'll be*

gone soon. "I knew you needed your rest to take care of Cora."

"A weak excuse at best. I'd have thought a man with your experience would have come up with a better line than that."

Ouch. Not helpless at all. "It's the truth."

She crossed her arms, perhaps unaware that the action threatened to topple her breasts from their crimson cage. "Let's get something straight, Dylan. I appreciate your helping me out in a bad situation. But I'm not going to get any crazy ideas. You've told me I don't belong in Silver Glen, and you're right. I'm not stupid enough to think that you and I are in some kind of relationship. So relax."

"Impossible," he muttered. "When I'm in the same room with you, relaxing is the last thing on my mind." He toyed with the seemingly innocuous crystal zipper pull. There was something intrinsically sexual about the damn thing. Gently, he lowered it two inches. Mia's sharply indrawn breath told him volumes. The curves of her pale breasts beckoned a man to touch, to worship.

When she didn't protest, he tugged again, this time uncovering her to the navel. "Lord, Mia," he said as his hand trembled. "You have the most incredible body. I can't stop thinking about last night."

Her head dropped backward. Her eyes closed as he traced the faint, silvery lines that marked places where her body had readied itself to give life. Slowly, he pushed the dress down her arms until it hung from her hips. Now she was naked from the waist up, a lush, erotic invitation. He gathered her close and held her, stroking her bare back.

They were standing in his brother's bedroom. Behind them a baby lay sleeping. Close by, a dinner party awaited their return. He shook with the urge to lift her against the wall and fill her. His erection was full and ready. Desire was a writhing, clawing beast inside him. He could lock the door. Pretend that Mia was still nursing Cora.

It was a measure of his desperation that he seriously considered it.

Instead, he released her and did the only thing left to him. Fisting one hand in her hair at the back of her head and using the other to tip up her chin, he kissed her roughly, forcefully. "Tonight, Mia. I want you again. And this time I won't leave." He wouldn't be able to, not again. He didn't have the will to walk away from something so perfect, even if the outcome would never fall in his favor.

Her arms twined around his neck. "Yes." The single word was a barely audible whisper.

He knew on some hazy, faraway level that they were crushing her dress. Imagining what she would look like if he helped her step out of it only made the ache in his gut worse.

Her lips were soft beneath his, unbearably sweet. For a split second he flashed back to that stolen kiss in high school, the one that had confused him and made him ashamed. Even then, there had been something about Mia that drew him. Some essential goodness that he sensed he lacked. As a seventeen-year-old, he'd known it, and he knew it now.

He didn't deserve a woman like this. He was selfish and focused on the here and now. Mia had a child to consider. She contributed to the greater good with her work. Frivolity wasn't in her repertoire. But perhaps in the short time she was with him he could teach her the benefits of being naughty once in a while.

When her small hands tugged at his shirttails and slipped beneath to settle on the bare skin at his waist, he flinched. He'd kept a tight rein on his libido this far, but feeling her fingers on him made his vision go fuzzy. "We have to stop," he said gruffly, cursing the situation and the lousy timing that ensured, at a minimum, a miserable hour ahead.

Mia moved her hands, now pushing against his chest. When she was free, she tugged at her dress, pink-cheeked.

At that very moment, a quiet knock sounded at the door and Liam's voice came softly. "Dessert and coffee on the table. You guys ready?"

Dylan brushed the hair from Mia's flushed cheeks. "On our way," he said. Carefully, he raised the zipper of her dress all the way to the top and smoothed her skirt with two hands. "You okay?" he asked, gazing at her intently. He couldn't read the secrets hidden in her eyes.

She nodded. "Let's go. They're waiting."

He allowed her to pass him, but at the last moment snagged her wrist and reeled her in for one last quick kiss. Thank God she was wearing smudge-proof lipstick. "I'm glad you came back to Silver Glen," he said, resting his forehead against hers.

"Me, too." She touched his cheek with a fleeting caress that made him shiver. "Me, too."

Mia had never been in such a situation. Dylan ushered her to the dining room, his hand at the small of her back. She felt exposed and embarrassed, but at the heart of it, disappointed that she and Dylan were not alone.

Zoe had made an angel food cake from scratch and topped it with a fresh strawberry compote. "Is Cora asleep?" she asked.

The question was innocent, but Mia blushed anyway, as if the three adults at the table knew exactly what she and Dylan had been up to. "She went down without a peep," Mia said, sitting down as Dylan took the chair to her right. "*Getting* her to sleep is never a problem. It's the two a.m. playtime that's killing me."

Maeve sat at the head of the table, Aidan at the foot.

The two couples occupied either side. Mia liked Maeve, though the woman's personality was one part steamroller and one part matriarch.

The older woman waved a hand. "Hang in there, my dear. I went through that with at least three of my boys. It will pass. In my experience, parenthood is an endurance test, a marathon where the stubborn win out in the end."

Mia laughed. "I hope you're right. But at this point, my chances of *winning* are no more than fifty-fifty at best."

Dylan interrupted. "Don't let Mia fool you. She's doing a wonderful job as a mother." He poured himself a cup of black coffee from a fancy silver pot. "Cora clearly is thriving."

Maeve focused her gaze on Mia. "So what will you do with Cora when you get a new job?"

There was no mistaking the note of disapproval. Mia felt her defenses go up, but tried to answer calmly. "I'll find a reputable day care, of course. There are quite a few good ones in the Raleigh/Durham area."

"Have you considered taking a leave? I know how hard it is to deal with an infant and be productive during the day."

It was Zoe's turn to jump into the conversation. Apparently she wasn't scared of her mother-in-law. "That's not always feasible, Maeve. Most women have to work outside the home. Particularly single moms. Not everyone has a fortune like the Kavanaghs. And besides, from what Liam has told me, Mia's work has far-reaching applications."

Mia gave Zoe a grateful smile. "I hope to find a balance that works for Cora and me. As much as I love my baby, my career is also important. I find it challenging and fulfilling. Ultimately, I think Cora will benefit from having a mother who uses her abilities and contributes to society. But I know that life is never perfect."

She saw the three brothers glance at each other. The

Kavanaghs had certainly known their share of heartache over the years. Losing a parent was never easy, and Reggie Kavanagh's body had never been recovered. Maeve had stepped into the breach, giving her boys all the love and support they needed to become successful adults. Perhaps she thought Mia was selfish to get pregnant as a single woman, because Maeve knew exactly how difficult it had been to be both mother *and* father. Mia wondered how the other brothers had fared in the absence of a male parent.

Dylan put an end to the awkward conversation. "I think Mia and I will call it a night. Zoe, the meal was fantastic. Feel free to try your culinary skills on me anytime."

Liam gave him a mock glare. "Quit flirting with my wife."

Dylan raised an innocent eyebrow. "Who, me?" As the group stood, he kissed Zoe on the cheek. "My brother is a Neanderthal. It's perfectly acceptable for men and women to be friends."

Zoe pinched his cheek. "You are such a rascal. Behave yourself and take Mia and little Cora home. I promise to feed you another day."

When Mia excused herself to put the baby in the infant carrier, she could hear the five Kavanaghs talking animatedly. Clearly they enjoyed spending time together. It made her realize that she wanted more children, at least one more. Cora would need a sibling, someone to have her back when life was hard. But in some corner of her heart, Mia knew that Cora needed a daddy as well. In all the struggle of trying to get pregnant, it had honestly not seemed like that big a deal.

Now, however, the truth stared her in the face. Seeing Dylan with Cora was an inescapable revelation. As she grew, Cora would want a father. And at some point, she would ask questions.

On a more practical note, having so much help with

Cora in recent days showed Mia that she was missing out on many things by trying to do it all herself. For a woman who was supposedly a genius, she had been woefully unprepared for the consequences of her actions.

As she gathered up her purse and the baby's accoutrements, Dylan came to help her carry Cora. They said their goodbyes and finally escaped into the hallway. Mia wondered if Maeve and Aidan were lingering with Liam and Zoe to discuss what was going on in Dylan's life and whether or not Mia was taking advantage of him.

In the elevator, Dylan was suspiciously quiet. Cora had stayed asleep through all the noisy goodbyes. Mia stared down at her skirt, trying not to remember how the fabric had pooled around her hips when Dylan half undressed her. She couldn't figure him out. At times he seemed intent on seducing her into his bed, and at others he kept his distance...almost as if Mia was a threat to him.

She wanted to talk to him during the ride home, but maybe there was nothing to say. He was a Kavanagh and she was a new mom with a baby and no real job at the moment. They had a tenuous connection at best, even though they had added a sexual component to their relationship.

Men liked sex. Men, as a rule, took sex when it was offered. What they did not do was give up their bachelor status without a fight.

Fortunately for Dylan, Mia had no intention of fighting. If she ever did get married, she wanted a man who wanted her. Completely. Brains and all. Dylan still wasn't comfortable with Mia knowing about his past struggles. If Mia's hunch was correct, no one in his family knew except for Maeve.

She wanted to whack him over the head and get him to admit that he was a smart man in all the ways that counted. But she had a feeling he wouldn't listen. Dylan was stubborn.

Her brain ran in circles searching for solutions. She couldn't turn her back on a lifetime of study and work that was significant and valuable. That would be selfish and irresponsible. But every day the prospect of staying in Silver Glen with Dylan held more and more allure.

As they neared the turn to his property, she took a deep breath, mentally gearing up for the evening ahead. In Liam and Zoe's bedroom, she and Dylan had seemed in perfect accord. But what would happen now?

Gertie had left lights on to welcome them home. For Mia, the sight of Dylan's beautiful house elicited much more than gratitude for the roof over her head. She loved the way he had made his place seem like part of the countryside. Privacy and seclusion created peace and a feeling of home in the deepest sense of the word.

For one fleeting second, she allowed herself to acknowledge the truth. She had feelings for Dylan Kavanagh. Messy, wonderful emotions that couldn't be organized in spreadsheets or analyzed by computer programs. Exhilaration and panic duked it out in her stomach.

Dylan had made Mia comfortable and welcome in his home. He had been charming and gentle with Cora. He had even tried to protect Mia from his desire for her, though that hadn't lasted long.

But what if she admitted she was equally hungry? Would it make a difference if she told him what she wanted? Was there a chance Dylan might want something more, as well?

She was in trouble either way. If his answer was no, she faced humiliation and hurt. But if his answer was yes, she faced another set of problems. Could she give up her career and be content as a wife and mother? No matter how wonderful living in Silver Glen might be, it would mean relinquishing an entire part of the life that had defined her since she'd become an adult.

Thirteen

Dylan scooped the infant seat out of the car and followed Mia up the stairs. Unlocking the front door while juggling a baby was a skill he hadn't known he possessed, but something about it was satisfying. Cora was so innocent, so perfect. It made him feel good to know that in some small way, he was helping protect her.

In deference to the sleeping child, they made their way across the living room without turning on additional lights. Mia had been remarkably quiet on the way home. He wondered if his mother's veiled criticisms had pissed her off. She'd be justified.

After they put Cora down and closed the door, he took Mia's hand. "Let's have some coffee and sit in front of the fire."

"It's late."

He lifted her fingers to his lips and kissed them. "Are you going to turn into a pumpkin?" She had already kicked off her shoes. The disparity in their heights emphasized the contrast of male to female.

Mia shrugged, her expression difficult to decipher. "I'll change and meet you in the kitchen."

"Don't," he said gruffly. "Don't change. Please. I have a few fantasies about this dress."

That brought a smile to her face. "It *is* a nice dress," she said, the words demure.

"Very user-friendly." He cupped a hand behind her neck and massaged the spot beneath her ear. "Maybe we don't need coffee." He'd never brought a lover to this house. Perhaps his social skills were rusty. Or maybe he was simply losing control.

Mia strained on her tiptoes to kiss him, her lips warm and eager against his. "I'm not at all thirsty," she said. "Maybe we should go to bed and get some rest."

"Rest?" He was befuddled by her scent and by the feel of silk beneath his fingertips. Silk fabric. Silky-skinned woman.

She drew him toward her bedroom. "We *will* rest. Afterward."

It boded well for him that Mia made no pretense of resistance. He liked not having to guess whether or not she wanted him. No mixed messages. No hidden agendas. Just a man and a woman sharing pleasure.

For a moment, he wanted to take her to *his* suite…to play sexy games on his turf. But there was Cora to consider, and besides, perhaps he would regret making erotic memories in his bed when Mia was gone.

Thinking about her departure gave him an uneasy feeling. So he shut down that particular train of thought and focused on the temptress in the red dress.

Once the bedroom door closed, Mia stepped away from him and seemed to lose her courage. She fidgeted.

He put his arm around her waist and walked her to the bed. Sitting on the edge of the mattress, he positioned her in front of him, still standing. "You are a beautiful woman, Mia Larin, but in this dress… Lord, have mercy. It's a good thing my heart's in good shape."

Her tense posture relaxed. "You're really good at that."

"At what?"

"Making a woman feel special."

"You *are* special," he insisted. There was doubt in her

eyes, so he set out to make a believer out of her. Tracing the edge of her bodice with a fingertip, he grinned when gooseflesh erupted on her bare arms. "Do I make you nervous, Mia?"

"A little." Her arms hung at her sides, but her fingers curled, indicating that she was not completely at ease.

"I'm the most amiable guy on the planet. No one is scared of me."

At last she moved. Running her thumb across his bottom lip, she knocked the breath out of him with her tender caress. "I don't have a great deal of experience with men, but you're different."

He didn't know whether to be pleased or annoyed. "That doesn't sound entirely like a compliment."

Her skin was pale in the dimly lit room, her dark-eyed gaze impossible to decipher. "I don't want to fall for a guy who has *carefree bachelor* tattooed across his libido." She ruffled his hair. "You make a woman want things you're not willing to give."

He felt a twinge of guilt. Mia wasn't wrong. "We never had any idea that this was anything more than fun."

"I know."

"And besides," he said, feeling defensive, "there's nothing for you here in Silver Glen. You know that."

"There's you." The absolute conviction in those two words rocked him on his heels.

His heart twisted…hard. She was making herself completely vulnerable to him, but he couldn't reciprocate. "I'm not anyone's prize. Trust me. If you want fun and games, I'm your man. But don't expect more from me than I can give, Mia. I thought you'd learned that lesson a long time ago."

Nothing on her face indicated that his blunt refusal of her unspoken request had hurt her. But she took a ragged little breath that could have meant anything. "You're honest. I'll give you that. I won't embarrass you anymore. Make love to me, Dylan."

He felt a lick of relief that she had dropped the subject, but at the same time a raw feeling he was closing a door that might never reopen. "I can do that." The words were forced from a tight throat.

That damned crystal beckoned him irresistibly. He toyed with it, the backs of his fingers stroking her cleavage. "I feel like it's Christmas morning and Santa brought me a special package wrapped in red."

The anticipation was almost more than he could take. But he wanted to draw out the pleasure until they were both drunk with it.

When he tugged at the faux jewel, the zipper gave easily. Too easily. He forced himself to stop at two inches.

Mia's eyes closed, her chest rising and falling with rapid breaths. "I swear I would have pegged you as one of those guys who rips off the paper to see what's inside."

He spanned her hips with his hands trying to decide if she was wearing panties. Surely so. His Mia was shy... though present evidence didn't support such a hypothesis.

"I am," he admitted. "But sometimes patience is a virtue."

"Not at the moment," she muttered.

He played with the clear stone again. Such a simple thing to torment a man—but oh-so-effective. Any other day, if he and Mia had shared more than a single encounter prior to tonight, he might have submitted to his caveman instincts and yanked the sparkly pull as far down as it would go in one rash movement. Even thinking about it gave him chills.

But he needed to work up to that. By her own admission, Mia was not widely experienced in the erotic arts. He didn't want to scare her by coming on too strong.

The zipper conceded another four inches. Now the dress

was in danger of falling. It clung to Mia's breasts tantalizingly, held there by nothing more than a whisper.

When he teased her tummy with a fingertip, he evoked a surprisingly strong reaction. Mia grabbed the top of her dress and held it close, her hand batting his away. "Stop that," she hissed. "I'm ticklish."

"I'll keep it in mind." Allowing her the pretense of holding him at bay, he took the zipper to its final destination. "Move your hands, Mia."

When she shook her head, a lock of dark, wavy hair fell over her almost bare shoulder. "You're still dressed," she protested.

"My turn will come." He grasped both of her wrists in one of his hands and held them away from her body. Gently, awkwardly—since he had only one hand to work with—he peeled the dress down her arms. Clearly, he hadn't thought this through, because Mia's bound wrists halted his progress. "Well, damn."

She had the audacity to laugh. "Now what? Maybe you're not as smooth an operator as I thought."

"You have a sassy mouth for someone who's supposed to be shy."

"I've changed, Dylan."

"I noticed."

The act of trapping her delicate wrists with one of his big hands had aroused him even more if that were possible. But his ultimate goal meant he had to release her in the short-term. Before she could grab the dress again, he took handfuls of the skirt and pulled. In a split second she was naked. Or almost. The tiniest pair of red undies covered only the essentials.

Mia took the poleaxed expression on Dylan's face as a good sign. "Are you window shopping?" she asked politely. He sat frozen, his gaze fixed on her underwear. The intensity of his gaze made her damp in a very intimate spot. Surely he couldn't tell.

Dylan cleared his throat. "Let's not ruin the dress."

He held her hand gallantly as she stepped out of it and tossed it toward a chair, not bothering to see if it landed properly. At the moment she was more interested in breaking Dylan free of his trance. Since he appeared to be stunned, she sat down beside him. "You've seen me naked before," she teased.

"Only once." He ran a hand from the middle of her thigh to her knee. His darker skin against hers made her shiver.

"I don't mean to criticize," she said, resting her head against his shoulder, "but there's a good chance Cora will be waking up soon. Do you mind if we speed this up?" She reached over and began unbuttoning his shirt with her right hand. Truthfully, she wouldn't mind if he made love to her with his tux on. Dylan was a younger, more handsome James Bond.

Or maybe she was a tad prejudiced.

Finally, he snapped out of it. His hand covered hers. "Stretch out on the bed, Mia."

It was an order. She took it as such, feeling ridiculously turned on by his air of authority. As she scooted toward the headboard, trying to act as if being mostly naked in front of a handsome man was the norm for her, Dylan stood with his hands on his hips and tracked her every move.

When she was settled, he tugged at his bowtie, beginning an unapologetic striptease entirely for her benefit. At least she assumed that was his intention. Maybe he just didn't like being rushed.

First he toed off his shoes and stripped off his socks. His trousers were next. The black silk boxers he wore did little to disguise his masculinity. His thrusting erection pushed out the fabric. His excitement was evident in the small wet spot near his waist.

He left the underwear in place and reached for the studs on his shirt. Instead of scattering them across the rug, he removed each one with painstaking slowness and dropped them into a glass dish on the dresser.

"Take the shirt off," she pleaded. If Cora woke up at this exact moment, Mia would die of frustration.

Dylan complied in silence, his eyes flashing, his face flushed.

When he was down to his one last item of clothing, she held out her hand. "Hurry. I can't wait anymore."

At last he showed some evidence of the impatience she was experiencing. He strode to the bed and came down beside her on one knee. "It was worth the trouble tonight of getting into a tux for the chance to see you in that dress. But without it, I think you're even more beautiful."

Before she could respond, he gathered her into his arms and rolled with her. Now she was on top with his silky drawers massaging her female bits. Shivers of anticipation raced up and down her spine. She rested her hands on his hard chest. Tonight he had looked every inch the wealthy, sophisticated Kavanagh.

Yet here, in the intimacy of her room and her bed, Dylan's true essence shone through. He could play the part of a civilized man about town when required. But the real Dylan, the bad boy she had met in high school, was this wild-eyed, feral male. Undomesticated. Determined to get what he wanted, no matter the cost.

She wasn't resisting. Why would she? Leaning down, supporting herself with one palm braced on his warm shoulder, she traced his jawline with her fingers, feeling the late-day stubble. "Your family loves you very much," she said. "And Liam and Aidan trust your opinions. I watched them tonight. They respect and admire you."

His smile was lopsided. "Not that I mind being buttered up, but what's your point?"

She felt his hands caress her butt. Did she really want to carry on a rational conversation at this particular juncture? "Never mind," she muttered. "It will keep." She wriggled her bottom, making Dylan groan.

Without second-guessing herself, she slid down in the bed and settled between his thighs. Licking gently, she dampened the silk that covered his sac. Dylan's back arched off the bed.

Panting, he fisted his hands in her hair. "I have a condom in my billfold," he croaked.

"You won't be needing that just yet."

Dylan's ragged curse ended in a moan as she gently bit his shaft through his boxers. She loved feeling him like this. His fiancée must have been insane to walk away from a man like Dylan.

It was clear his patience was at an end when he put his hands under her arms and dragged her upward for a hot, punishing kiss. "You're a heartless tease," he accused.

"All the better to seduce you, my dear."

He went still. "Is that who I am? A notch on your bedpost?"

"What does that mean?" Irritated, she pulled away.

He lay there like a great cat, his tawny skin radiating heat as he stared at her with an unreadable gaze. "You move in academic circles with men whose intellects are equal to yours. Is what we're doing here your walk on the wild side?"

She scowled, the impulse to slap him almost winning. "That's insulting to both of us. I thought we were having fun. Clearly I was wrong." Furious, she scrambled away from him, intent on fleeing.

But Dylan had other ideas. One strong hand grasped her ankle and pulled her back. He sat up, gripping her shoulders and shaking her gently. "I needed to know the truth, Mia."

Tears stung her eyes, but she blinked them back. "Why?"

His jaw worked. "I've been used before. I didn't particularly enjoy it."

"Well, I *am* using you," she cried. "Though maybe not in the way you're thinking. You're housing and feeding my daughter and me. You're paying me to do a job that any one of a dozen people in Silver Glen could have handled easily. So what does that make *me?* I've hit rock bottom. If I wanted to make love to you, it sure as hell had nothing to do with scoring some imaginary coup."

Their faces were mere inches apart, his breath warm on her cheek. She could see his long, thick lashes and the way they framed his beautiful, intense eyes.

He kissed her lazily. "Fair enough. I should have known you couldn't resist my animal magnetism."

Resting her forearms on his shoulders, she linked her hands behind his neck and played with his hair. "Modesty isn't one of your strong suits, is it?"

"I'm cursed with being irresistible to women."

His tongue-in-cheek humor restored her equilibrium. "Thank God you have me to take you down a peg or two. Otherwise, your head would be too big to get through the door."

"Hold that thought."

He rolled away long enough to get rid of his boxers and to grab protection. Though the banter was lighthearted, his expression was anything but. Standing beside the bed, he rolled latex over his straining shaft.

When he returned, settling on his knees in front of her, it was clear that the time for talking was past. He touched her intimately, checking her readiness. She was mortifyingly wet. Wanting Dylan was a living, breathing ache.

She rested her forehead against his shoulder. "I need you," she whispered.

Lowering her carefully onto her back, he moved over

her with purpose, fitting the head of his erection to her center and pushing with a firm thrust. She inhaled sharply, her mind spinning in a dozen directions.

The confidence of his possession was warranted. His knowledge of a woman's body guaranteed satisfaction. Mia realized he was bringing her to the brink in record time. She savored the physical connection, convinced that Dylan was the only man who ever had or ever would be able to touch her so deeply, so well.

The room was quiet, save for the sounds of his exertion. Whatever veneer of polish he had donned for the evening with his family was stripped away, incinerated in the heat of their coupling. She wrapped her legs around his waist. "Don't stop," she begged, spiraling upward toward an invisible peak.

"Never."

It was a futile request and an unrealistic answer. The force of their need reduced them to the most basic human level. She bit his neck, marking him as hers. His skin was damp with sweat. Her mouth was dry.

Suddenly, he cried out, his big body shuddering atop hers. What sent her over the edge was the realization that for this one moment in time, Dylan wanted her and needed her.

For now, it was enough.

Fourteen

Sometime in the wee hours of the morning, a sound woke Dylan. He lay still for a moment, processing the fact that he was not in his own bed. Then everything came rushing back. His sex stirred reflexively, stimulated by the memories.

The sound came again. He reared up on one elbow long enough to observe the monitor. Cora was stirring.

Stealthily, he slid out of bed, anxious to catch the baby before she awakened Mia.

Cora gave him an adorable toothless smile when he bent over her crib. "Hey, sweet cheeks." The way she looked at him made it clear that she already recognized the man in the house. When he picked her up and snuggled her, the baby smell entranced him. He realized in an instant that he had fallen in love with Cora. The sensation that gripped his chest was a simple, entirely natural emotion, but a profound one.

As he changed her diaper, she kicked her feet and cooed. Blowing a raspberry on her chubby tummy, he felt his heart turn over. She was so sweet and perfect. And she deserved a father.

The knowledge made him uncomfortable. He knew his limitations. What would it be like if he ever had a child of his own, and Dylan were unable to help with homework? Or even worse, what if the kid took after him?

Cora would be smart. He knew it. But Cora and Mia were a package. If he couldn't keep Mia, the baby wasn't his either. Wrapping the infant in a thin cotton blanket against the chill of the air-conditioning, he carried her into the bedroom and sat down on Mia's side of the bed. Touching her hip through the covers, he shook he gently. "Someone wants her mama," he said quietly.

Mia sat up, shoving the hair from her face. She was nude. The realization seemed to take her by surprise, because she flushed and scrambled for the safety of the bathroom.

Dylan kissed the baby's cheek. "Don't worry. She'll be back."

When Mia returned moments later, she was covered neck to toe in a thin black robe made of a soft knit that clung to her body. With her hair tumbled down around her shoulders, she looked like a sexually sated woman. She settled herself back in bed without looking at Dylan and reached for the baby. "You should have woken me up. Cora isn't your responsibility."

He stood for a moment, watching as the baby rooted for a nipple. "I love your daughter," he said flatly. "Nothing about caring for her is a chore."

Pissed for no good reason, he returned to his side of the bed and climbed under the covers, sprawling on his back. With one arm flung across his face, he listened to Cora's enthusiastic nursing. Occasionally, Mia murmured to her daughter. Although the tenor of the words was soft and affectionate, he couldn't actually make out what Mia said.

He was almost asleep when she addressed *him*.

Perhaps Cora was nodding off already, because Mia's words were a whisper. "When Cora gets in school, will you think less of her if she has learning difficulties?"

The out-of-nowhere question jerked him from the edge of slumber. "Of course not."

"So you won't think she's stupid or slow?"

Suddenly, he saw where this was going. "No," he said. "I won't."

He didn't need any further explanation to get what Mia was trying to tell him. He had worn the hair shirt of his academic failures stubbornly, unable to see past his youthful struggles. The truth was, he wasn't that high-school boy anymore. Sure, he still had trouble with numbers and letters, and he always would. But what did that matter?

Suddenly, the ridiculous irony of their situation slapped him in the face. Mia had used an "average" sperm donor so she wouldn't have a child as smart as she was. Dylan was unwilling to father a child who might struggle in school as he had. Unwittingly, he and Mia were trying to play God.

Neither of them had asked to be born with a high IQ or a reading disorder. They had both played the hands they'd been dealt. It was long past time to move on.

He'd used his frustrating studies as a yardstick to measure his success, but Mia was right. He had a lot to be proud of. The Silver Dollar drew customers from miles around and was a stopping-off point for those who wanted to explore the town. His family was close and supportive. He had a wide circle of friends and a house he'd designed from the ground up, a place of respite and peace at the end of the day.

Everything a man could want or need was his. Except for a wife. And a baby. Mia and Cora fit the bill more perfectly than any two people he could have conjured up in his imagination. There were obstacles. He'd be the first to admit it. But he loved Mia. Her job and her talent had kept him from admitting it. Now he acknowledged the truth.

He had believed he wasn't good enough for her. But maybe love was the one ability that trumped all the rest. He could offer Mia things she had never found with other men. And by God, he was going to make her believe it. The joyous possibilities swelled in his chest, though he tempered his enthusiasm, unwilling to tip his hand too soon.

His heart thudded in his chest. Was he really contemplating such an enormous change in his life?

As Mia shifted Cora to her other breast with a smile for her infant daughter, he knew that his answer was yes. Mia brought something unique to his home and to his life. Excitement, yes. But also a deep sense of satisfaction. When he was with her, he felt at peace. Which was odd, because until Mia and Cora arrived in Silver Glen, Dylan would have sworn that his life was perfect as it was.

Imagining his house without them, even after such a short time, was unthinkable. Here in Mia's bed, he realized that what he had shared with his ex-fiancée had been ephemeral at best. It was the difference between a flesh-and-blood woman and a hologram. Tara had been a chameleon, playing a part even when the cameras weren't rolling.

Mia was exactly the opposite. She was real and grounded and complete. Even with his eyes closed, he knew the moment when she got up to carry Cora back to her crib. Moments later the covers rustled as she climbed back in bed, this time staying far to her side of the mattress.

Despite the late hour and their need for sleep, a stronger need drove him. In the dark he donned a condom and then took her arm and urged her closer, meeting her in the middle of the bed. Mia came willingly. She was naked again—soft and warm and so intensely feminine in his arms. He was beginning to learn the touches that pleased her, the little catches of breath that told him he had found a sensitive spot.

Though his hunger for her was as fierce as it had been in the beginning, he didn't mount her at first. Instead, he reveled in the feel of her body pressed against him. Her legs tangled with his. Her hands pulled his head down for a kiss that was equal parts passion and play.

"You amaze me," he muttered.

"It's the testosterone talking." She slid her fingers into his hair, making him shiver. "I'm a rookie. Maybe it's beginner's luck."

Though she turned his rough praise into a joke, he had never been more serious. Parting her thighs with his hand, he moved between her legs and entered her slowly. Someone sighed. Maybe her. Maybe him. This time, there was no rush.

In the darkness, he could pretend this was all that mattered. This heady rush of physical bliss. This feeling that he was in control of his domain. That all was right with the world.

Mia came before he did, her orgasm a gentle rolling wave. He picked up the pace of his thrusts and followed her, welcoming the now familiar physical release that racked him and turned him inside out.

In the aftermath, he heard her breathing settle into an even cadence. In moments she would be asleep.

"Mia." He whispered near her ear, his lips brushing her temple.

"Hmm?" She was tucked into his embrace with her bottom nestled against his groin. It was time to yield to slumber, not to talk, but this couldn't wait.

"When the apartment over the Silver Dollar has been repaired, I don't want you and Cora to move. I want you to stay here."

He couldn't miss the way her body stiffened.

"Why?" she asked.

Because I like having you under my roof and in my bed.

That kind of declaration was a lot to throw at a woman in the middle of the night, so he backpedaled. "I think it would be better for Cora to have some continuity. She's already moved once, and she seems to like it here. Besides, I have a yard for her to play in."

"She's only three months old, Dylan. We'll leave Silver Glen before she even starts walking."

"I care about you," he said baldly, his hands shaking. "And about Cora. My house is still a healthier atmosphere for a baby than a cramped apartment over a bar. Promise me you'll think about it."

Her head pillowed on his arm, she yawned. "I care about you, too, Dylan. So I'll consider it. I promise. Go to sleep now. We can talk about this tomorrow."

When Mia woke up the next morning, Dylan was gone. Again. But this time, she knew he had spent the night in her bed. Shortly before dawn, he'd made love to her one last time.

It was anybody's guess as to where he was at the moment.

After pulling on clean undies and her robe, she went to fetch Cora, her limbs protesting every step. Much of her body was pleasantly sore, but any discomfort she experienced was offset by an almost palpable sense of well-being. She felt satiated and smug.

Dylan had told her he cared about her. It was a lot from a man who guarded himself so carefully. And she had been brave enough to reciprocate without worrying about getting hurt.

Cora was not a great conversationalist, but Mia engaged her anyway. "Dylan wants us to stay, little one. He loves you and he likes me. So we're going to enjoy the moment. Okay with you?" She took the baby's chortle as a sign of agreement.

Glancing at her watch, she decided to prevail on Gertie's good nature once again. She found the older woman occupying her customary morning post, frying bacon and scrambling eggs. "Good morning, Gertie."

"I suppose it is," Gertie said with a grin. "Did the baby sleep?"

"She did. One brief feeding in the middle of the night, but that was it, thank goodness."

The housekeeper set a plate on the table and motioned to Mia. "Eat it while it's hot." Mia, with the baby on her lap, wolfed down a double serving of both bacon *and* eggs and topped it off with one of Gertie's homemade biscuits and jam. It was embarrassing how hungry she was. Normally a cup of yogurt and some coffee would see her through the morning, but after last night's sexual excess, she was starving.

When Gertie finished up the last of the bacon and set it on a paper towel to drain, Mia suddenly realized that Dylan might not have eaten yet. Casually, she took a sip of her orange juice and fished for information. "Did Dylan head into town already?"

Gertie shook her head. "Nope. He's out back getting the boys started."

"The boys?"

"He gives jobs to boys in the foster-care system. Mostly yard work and the like. And he tells them if he ever catches them spending their paychecks on drugs, he'll tear them limb from limb."

"And they believe him?"

"Oh, yes. Mr. Dylan can be fierce when he needs to be. Everyone sees him as this laid-back, good-natured fellow, but he's got strong opinions and strong beliefs about right and wrong. Look how he brought you and the baby here to his house. He could have settled you in a motel room somewhere, but that wouldn't have been right. That boy's moral compass points due north. I know his mama raised her sons to be responsible, but Dylan takes it a step farther. He's a gentleman and a provider. He'll always look out for the weak and the helpless and the ones who've been given hard knocks."

As Mia finished her breakfast, she felt some of her euphoria winnow away. In the middle of the night when Dylan had asked her to stay longer than originally planned, her heart had flipped in her chest. Mentally, she had heard the word *care* as *love*. Dylan wanted to get closer to her. He wanted to pursue their burgeoning relationship, sexually and otherwise.

Now, in the cold light of day, and with Gertie's passionate analysis of Dylan's personality, it seemed more than likely that Dylan's invitation had been the result of altruism. Her mood deflated like a cheap balloon. She gave herself a mental pep talk. Nothing had changed. Cora and Mia still had a home. Mia had a job.

Best of all, Mia was sharing Dylan's bed for the moment. She had never expected more than that. So why was she now feeling disappointed and low?

Wiping her mouth with an elegant cloth napkin, she gave Gertie a beseeching smile. "Would you mind playing with her for twenty minutes while I grab a quick shower?"

"You know the answer to that." Gertie took the baby with alacrity. "Go do what you need to do. Me and this little lady will entertain each other."

Mia crossed the house toward the wing that housed her suite and Dylan's. As she passed his doorway, an unwelcome thought occurred. When Gertie went to tidy her boss's room and make his bed, she would see that the bed hadn't been slept in. The woman was smart enough to put two and two together. Surely she would guess that Dylan had been in another bed. Very close by.

Stealthily, Mia opened Dylan's door. She had never been inside. The furnishings and decor were equally as luxurious as hers, but the colors were more masculine.

Lots of navy and burgundy. Rapidly, she went to the huge bed and threw back the covers, twisting them until they looked like the remnants of a good night's sleep.

One by one, she plumped the pillows. She even knocked one onto the floor for good measure. Satisfied that she had done her best, she turned to leave and ran smack into the bed's owner.

"Dylan," she squeaked, feeling as guilty as if he had caught her raiding his safe.

The flash of white teeth in his broad grin added further color to her hot cheeks. "Whatcha doin', little Mia?" He crossed his arms over his chest. Since he was blocking her only exit, his stance surely wasn't coincidental.

"I, uh…" Well, shoot, she might as well fess up. "I didn't want Gertie to know you hadn't slept in your bed."

His lips twitched, but he didn't laugh. "I'm a grown man," he said, his voice deceptively mild considering the predatory gleam in his eyes. "Gertie doesn't weigh in on my sleep habits."

Before she could defend herself with additional rational explanations, Dylan reached out and stripped her out of the thin robe she wore.

She shrieked and batted at his hands. "Are you nuts? We're not alone."

With a calm she couldn't emulate, he turned and locked his door. "Gertie took the baby for a walk. I want you again, Mia."

The even tenor of his words didn't match the hot, intent gaze that took in every inch of her body. She didn't know why she was embarrassed. He had seen it all last night. Had touched it and kissed it and…

He cut short her mental gyrations by scooping her into his arms. But he didn't walk toward the bed. Instead, he pushed her against the nearest wall. Her legs went around his waist automatically. "Dylan, we can't." It was a weak protest at best, and he took it as such.

"A quickie, Mia. You've heard the term, I'm sure." Without letting her fall, he unbuckled his belt, unzipped his pants and freed his stiff erection. After one-handedly rolling on a condom, he bit her earlobe. "Hang on, honey. This is going to be hard and fast."

Before she could utter a word, he reached between her legs, thrust aside the thin cotton crotch of her undies and pushed inside her, all the way to the hilt.

Beyond the window, Mia could hear the voices of the young men working in the yard. Birds sang. A lawnmower roared. But in Dylan's beautifully appointed bedroom, there was no talking. He took her roughly, urgently, as if it had been months instead of hours since they had mated. His breath smelled of coffee. He tasted like bacon and orange marmalade. His big, tough body held her aloft easily.

She hadn't been prepared for this. No foreplay. No wooing. Which made it all the more mortifying when she climaxed wildly, even before Dylan had finished. The culmination of her pleasure galvanized him. Ramming into her with low groans, he jerked and cursed when his own release found him moments later.

Mia knew her bottom would be sore tomorrow from being pummeled against the wall. But she couldn't seem to care. The novelty of having a man go insane with lust in her presence was a powerful analgesic.

Dylan cleared his throat. "Should I apologize?" he asked, the words rueful.

She pressed her hand over his wildly beating heart. "I don't know. Maybe you should do it again so I can be sure."

Fifteen

Dylan was in over his head. In high school, as a popular kid with lots of money, getting girls had never been a problem. Fortunately, he'd had the good sense to use appropriate protection. But teenage sex and sex in his early twenties had been more about physical release than about bonding with any particular female.

He considered himself a generous lover. None of his partners had ever complained, not even Tara, who had appeared to enjoy his bed but not enough to stay. By the time he met her, he'd been old enough to actually consider settling down. She had flattered his ego. And he had been suckered into the fantasy.

But he had been naive. Fortunately, his broken engagement no longer gave him sleepless nights. He'd made a mistake. And he was lucky it hadn't taken him as far as the altar. Tara was firmly in the past.

Mia, on the other hand, managed to combine the past and the present in one confusing amalgam of nostalgia and sexual hunger.

Instead of releasing her, he carried her to his bathroom, knowing she would want to freshen up before she sneaked across the hall to the safety of her own bedroom. When he set her on her feet, he managed a smile, even though he was in no way sanguine about had just happened.

To be honest, he was pretty much a vanilla guy when

it came to sex. He liked sex. A lot. And often was always better than not at all. But Mia had done something to him. She'd made him feel a gnawing hunger that was not exactly comfortable. In fact, his response to her was pretty damned alarming. How could a meek, quiet, unassuming female turn him inside out and make him doubt everything he'd ever known about himself?

"Mia," he said, unable to keep quiet. "Are you going to stay? For now?"

At the moment, she clutched her robe to her chest with white-knuckled fingers. What she didn't know was that in the mirror he could see the outline of her cute heart-shaped butt through the thin fabric. Clenching his fists to keep from reaching for her again, he leaned against the doorframe. "I'd like an answer please."

When she smiled at him, his legs went weak. "Yes, Dylan. For now."

He cleared his throat, concealing the rush of jubilation evoked by her quiet agreement. "Good." He paused. "It's a gorgeous day outside. What if we get Gertie to fix us a picnic?"

"Cora, too?"

"Of course. She's part of the package."

"That would be nice."

Mia's eyes were huge. He noticed her gaze drop briefly to his pants where his fly was still open. Calmly, he tucked in his shirt, adjusted the rest of his clothing and hoped she didn't notice that he was still semierect.

"I'll go talk to her now," he said. "Let me know when you're ready."

"But we just ate breakfast."

"I'll throw in a tour of the house before we go. And there are things in the woods I want you to see."

"Sounds like the script for a horror movie."

He laughed out loud. Considering that he had to spend

the better part of the next three days dealing with construction headaches down at the Silver Dollar, he knew he deserved this outing. Mia's company was icing on the cake and then some.

Mia was grateful when Dylan disappeared. After one disbelieving look in the mirror, she straightened her hair, carefully fastened the sash of her robe and then returned to her own room to shower and dress. Since Dylan had given her a heads-up, she packed a diaper bag for Cora, and then chose for herself an outfit that was comfortable and suited to the outdoors.

The amber knit top and faded jeans were around-the-house clothing, but after she put her hair in a ponytail and slicked some lip gloss across her mouth, she didn't look half bad. Her canvas espadrilles were made more for style than for walking in the great outdoors, but they would do.

By the time she made it back to the kitchen, her twenty minutes had mushroomed to thirty-five. Since she couldn't explain why she was late, she decided it was better not to say anything at all.

Gertie and Cora were just coming in the back door when Mia found them. The baby threw out her arms when she saw her mama.

Mia took her, holding her tight. It never ceased to amaze her that her love for this little girl grew every day. "Come here, angel. Were you good for Miss Gertie?"

"Best baby I ever saw. Mr. Dylan asked me to put together a picnic. Any special requests?"

Mia shook her head. "Everything you make is wonderful. I've been avoiding spicy food since I'm nursing, but other than that, the menu is wide-open as far as I'm concerned."

Dylan joined them, his presence making the large

kitchen seem to shrink. "While Gertie is organizing our picnic, why don't I show you the upstairs?"

She didn't confess that she had already snooped. "Sounds good to me."

The guest rooms on the second floor were exquisite. "I had help with the furnishings and decor," Dylan confessed.

Each one was different and beautiful in its own way. "You must enjoy having company," she said.

"I do. Several of the guys I went to high school with have moved away. It's fun to host them and their families when they come back for visits to Silver Glen."

"And single women?" Mia gave him a wry look, knowing the answer to that one.

But Dylan surprised her. "If you mean girlfriends, the answer is no. I've never had a lover here."

"Not even Tara?" She raised an eyebrow.

"I lived in a condo in town when I was engaged to Tara. It was after we broke up that I built this place. It's my personal space. My retreat, I guess you'd call it."

"And yet you brought Cora and me here."

He shrugged. "No choice really."

"There's always a choice in life. You could have put us up in a hotel. Why didn't you?"

"I owed you something. For the past. And besides, Cora wormed her way into my heart."

"And me?"

His gaze settled on her mouth, hungry...wanting. "Let's just say that what I feel for you now is a wee bit different than it was in high school. C'mon," he said, taking her arm. His fingers were warm against her skin. She was so attuned to his touch that she felt little sizzles and sparks fizz through her bloodstream. It was impossible to be so close to him and not remember other things. More private things.

He led her to a door at the end of the hall.

"Another bedroom?" she asked.

"Nope. This is the attic access. Let me carry Cora. The steps are steep."

She trusted him implicitly with her daughter. And she was glad he had offered his help. The stairs were indeed slanted sharply upward.

When they reached the top, Dylan flipped a light switch. The cavernous, unfinished space smelled of wood shavings and dust. Cobwebs caught the light. "I'm not sure what we're looking at," she said. If this were a romantic tryst, he wouldn't have brought a baby along.

Handing Cora back to her, he cranked a large handle. Gradually, a section of the roof began to open. Now, with the sunlight pouring in, she saw a large telescope against the far wall. "It's a makeshift observatory," he said, clearly enthused about his revelation. "I come up here on clear nights and look at the stars. That's why I bought this property. We're far enough away from town to escape the light pollution."

"Where did you get the telescope? And how did you learn to use it?"

"I took a class online. Ordered the parts. Put it together."

"Dylan." The exasperation in her voice got through to him.

"What?" He seemed genuinely perplexed.

"I don't want to hear another damn word about how smart I am or how dumb you are. Are we clear?"

Dylan shrugged, grinning. "Yes, ma'am."

Poor Cora seemed baffled by her mother's rant.

Mia felt better for having that off her chest, but she realized that yelling at the man she was falling for probably wasn't the smartest tack to take.

Before she could apologize for her vehemence, an unexpected crack of thunder made all three of them jump.

A large summer storm cloud had come out of nowhere, it seemed, and suddenly the sky above was gray and roiling. The wind picked up, and they felt the first drops of rain.

Dylan manned the crank with all his might, closing the gap just in time to prevent the attic from being soaked. It was quieter suddenly, and awkward.

He put his hands in his back pockets. She saw his chest rise and fall. Sometimes she forgot how handsome he was. Looking at him now, she tried to see him through a stranger's eyes. Some people would write him off as a simple guy with a gift for gab and a charming smile. But there was so much more to Dylan. In that instant, she knew that her feelings were far more involved than was wise. She wished she knew what he was thinking. "I guess that's it for our picnic," she said.

"We could have it in the living room in front of the fireplace. I'm sure Gertie can rustle up an old blanket for us. Cora would like that, wouldn't she?"

"Of course."

Dylan busied himself carrying things from the kitchen to the living room, but he reeled mentally. Mia had read him the riot act upstairs in the attic. And she seemed so adamant that she was right. Had he really been so clueless about his own abilities? Had he allowed an unspoken competition with his older brother to make him feel inadequate?

As he settled onto the quilt with Mia and Cora, he had to smile. Awash in contentment, he listened as the storm raged in full fury. Rain lashed the windows in wind-driven sheets. Gertie, watching the radar, had decided to make a run for home half an hour ago, hoping to miss the worst of the weather. She didn't live far. Dylan was sure she had made it without much trouble, but he sent a text just in case and was reassured when she replied that she was home safe and sound.

Mia had said very little during their informal meal. In fact, she had addressed most of her attention toward Cora. Unfortunately for Mia, the baby was fast succumbing to sleep. Dylan, without asking, tucked sofa pillows around her so she wouldn't roll into anything hurtful as she slept.

When he was done, he crouched beside Mia and stroked her cheek. "Has the cat got your tongue?"

Her abashed look was adorable. "I shrieked at you like a fish wife," she said, her expression remorseful. "I'm sorry."

He drew her down onto the quilt, leaning against the low wall in front of the hearth and putting her head in his lap. "I'm actually flattered. And I'll concede, you may have a point."

After that, they were quiet, content to listen to the storm outside and the crackle of the fire close by. He combed his fingers through her hair, wondering if he would always remember this day as a turning point in his life. He knew what he wanted now. Mia. For always. And Cora. And maybe—when he'd had time to get used to the idea—a second kid.

There was still the matter of Mia's work. To be honest, he couldn't imagine ever leaving Silver Glen. But when it came down to it, he was more sure every moment that he would choose Mia and Cora over most anything else he could think of.

He touched her cheek. "What are you thinking about?

When she looked up at him, he could swear he saw something in her eyes that reflected what was in his heart. For a long time he thought she wasn't going to answer him. But finally, she spoke.

"I was thinking about how lucky I was to come to Silver Glen and run into you again. My life was in chaos, but you were so calm and reassuring. For the first time I began to think that Cora and I were going to make it."

"Of course you were going to make it. You're a bright, capable woman. But everyone needs help once in a while."

She sat up. "Is that the only reason we're together? Because you like helping damsels in distress?"

He cupped her face in his hands. "It was my pleasure to do whatever I could for you and Cora. But no. We're together because of a magnetic attraction. You must have learned about that in science class."

Nibbling his fingers, she smiled wryly. "So you're calling this thing between us *opposites attract?*"

He kissed her softly and released her, unwilling to let things get out of hand with the baby nearby. "We're not opposites at all, Mia. Not where it really counts. We both value family. And roots. You wanted that connection badly enough to have a baby on your own."

Desire shimmered between them. They were enclosed in an intimate cocoon courtesy of the storm and the fire and the memories of last night and this morning.

Mia cocked her head, her expression reflecting his own physical need. "Cora is asleep."

He felt his neck heat. "We can't leave her here. And if we try to move her, she might wake up."

"I was thinking about how comfortable your sofa is."

His eyes darted to the furniture in question. He swallowed hard. "Really?" It was not a question about the couch.

Mia understood. "Really."

He helped her to her feet and held her hand as they crossed the thick carpet to the long, leather-covered divan. In hushed silence, they undressed each other. Shirts and pants. Socks and shoes. Unlike the night that cloaked activities in secret, this was the middle of the afternoon.

There was no hiding, metaphorical or otherwise. Mia's

gaze held his steadily, though he could see remnants of her innate shyness. When he knelt and drew her last piece of clothing down her legs, she stepped out of the lacy panties and stood before him bare as the day she was born.

He shed his boxers and felt a rush of heat scald his spine when Mia immediately took his shaft in her hands and stroked him from root to tip. He saw wonder in her eyes, the same wonder he felt. How could two such different people find common ground in such a primeval way?

The bare leather sofa seemed cold to the touch, so he grabbed a soft mohair afghan and spread it across the cushions. "Ladies first," he said.

When she stretched out and propped her foot on the back of the couch, the bottom fell out of his stomach at the sheer eroticism of the view. After rapidly taking care of protection, he came down on top of her, bracing himself on one arm to spare her his weight. Thunder still boomed overhead, rattling panes of glass in the windows. Mia had been silent through it all.

"I need this," he croaked, almost beyond speech. "I need you."

Her small, winsome smile warmed him from the inside out. "Then we're both going to get what we want."

He wanted to ask her to stay forever. To walk away from her old life. But that seemed incredibly selfish. So he tried to show her with his body that she was special to him. Ignoring the blistering urge to mate, he paid homage to her quiet beauty. Lingering kisses at her throat. Sharper nips at her collarbone.

Soon, though, Mia was not content to be passive. She found his mouth and kissed him recklessly. "I won't break, Dylan. And I don't want to wait. Let me feel you inside me."

It was an invitation he couldn't refuse. Bending her knee to gain access, he positioned himself. "I want to go on record as saying that I'm working under adverse conditions."

He watched as Mia stifled her giggle, biting her lip. "Duly noted," she whispered.

When he entered her, they went from amusement to awe. Eyes open, locked on hers, he moved inside her, feeling his world shift on its axis. Nothing in his life had ever felt so right, so natural. "Mia…" He had no clue what he was trying to say.

She held his gaze bravely, her arms linked around his neck. "I know, Dylan. I know."

How long it lasted, he couldn't say. A minute. An hour. A handful of seconds. Everything faded away. At last, even looking at her became too much of an effort. He closed his eyes, concentrating. Her sex gripped his, making him sweat.

The sofa creaked beneath the force of his movements. Wooly fibers scratched his legs. Sliding his hand beneath Mia's butt, he lifted her into his thrusts, hearing the choked inarticulate cries that told him she was close.

So sweet…she was so damned sweet and sexy.

Without warning, something inside him snapped. Wildly he plunged into her, straining for the goal and yet trying to hold back an inescapable tide. "Mia, Mia," he groaned.

The end, when it came, was swift, incredible and draining.

As he collapsed on top of her, he heard her whisper something, but his heart beat too loudly in his ears for him to hear.

Sixteen

Mia found herself in a predicament for which none of her studies had prepared her. She was in love with a man who clung stubbornly to the idea that she was only passing through. And for the life of her, she couldn't tell him he was wrong, though more and more every day, she wanted to. What Dylan offered was unbearably sweet. But it would mean giving up a great deal. And her sacrifice was predicated on the assumption that he wanted her for the long haul.

His weight was a pleasant burden. She honestly could not tell if he was asleep or not, but the momentary quiet gave her time to think. In her estimation, the sex they had shared was more than just momentarily satisfying. Their physical intimacy seemed born of a deeper connection.

Dylan's tenderness made her believe he cared even more than he had admitted to her.

But was she deceiving herself?

Moments later, Dylan stirred, lifting off her and standing up. The eye-level view of his sex was disconcerting.

He pulled her to her feet, tucking her against his chest. "We need to talk, Mia." His big body was warm and hard, making her feel both safe and aroused at the same time, a dangerous combination.

Her heart stuttered. "About what?"

"You. Me. Us."

"Okay." Her face was buried in his chest. To look at him would have taken more courage than she had at the moment. Her hands rested decorously at his waist, but she badly wanted to stroke his firm buttocks. The tone of his voice could have meant anything, but considering the way his erection nudged her abdomen, she had to hope that this *talk* was going to be a good thing.

Chilled suddenly, and more than a little embarrassed about their nudity in broad daylight, she stepped back, folding her arms across her breasts. "I need to clean up and get dressed. Cora will want to eat soon. Patience isn't her strong suit."

Dylan stood with his feet braced, shoulders squared, as he covered her from head to toe with a hot gaze. His smile made her toes curl. "It's probably for the best. Otherwise we might spend the whole day screwing our brains out."

"Dylan!"

He held up his hands. "Sorry. I'm weak and you're irresistible."

"No, I'm not." His praise made her heart sing, but she tried to keep her feet firmly planted on the ground.

"I'll be the judge of that." He glanced at the clock on the mantel. "If you don't mind being alone here with Cora, I really should run into town and see if the storm did any damage to the building. The insurance company had a tarp installed over the roof, but I don't know if it held in the wind."

"We'll be fine."

"I want to take you to dinner up at the hotel tonight. Table for two. Very private. So we can talk about your future. Our future."

She shivered inwardly, hoping for a miracle. "I'd like that. But what about Cora?"

"I'm pretty sure Zoe would love to babysit for a couple of hours, but I'll call her as I drive into town and check."

Mia picked up her clothes and held them in front of her. Dylan appeared entirely comfortable in his nakedness and in no hurry to rush off. She was not quite so sanguine. So she changed the subject. "At some point today or tomorrow morning I need you to glance at the forms I filled out for your quarterly tax report. I haven't submitted it yet because I wanted you to take a look and see if it's okay."

"I'm sure it's fine, but if it will make you feel better…"

"Thanks."

He took pity on her physical paralysis. "Go get dressed. I'll make sure Cora's okay until you get back."

As Dylan watched her walk away, he enjoyed the rear view. Making love to Mia was a revelation. She had more passion hidden beneath her quiet, reserved personality that anyone he had ever met. Tonight he would tell her he loved her and feel her out about the possibility of staying in Silver Glen permanently.

He was not fooling himself. There was a better-than-even chance that his relationship might not make it to September. Autumn in the Carolina mountains was spectacular. By then the bar would be up and running, and he would have something to distract him from the pain if Mia decided she couldn't stay.

And it would be pain. He already knew that. Hopefully, he was prepared for it.

He dressed rapidly and picked up Cora as she cried out. The baby looked up at him with eyes that were so much like her mother's. For a moment, Dylan felt sympathy for the anonymous man who would never know this precious child.

Being a father was about more than planting a seed. It meant sharing sleepless nights, dealing with croup and strep throat, and reading up on ways to care for diaper rash. *Daddy* was a full-time job, but one with enormous benefits. Being with Cora had changed him…or at least opened his eyes. He would do anything for that kid.

During tonight's dinner, he would lay out his plan. If Mia was on the same page, perhaps during the next few months they could decide if it was possible to mesh their lives.

When Mia reappeared, his heart donkey-kicked him in the chest. He spoke gruffly to cover the emotion that threatened to choke him. "I'm leaving now." He handed over the warm bundle of baby fat and drooling smiles. "Unless you hear otherwise, we'll plan on leaving at six."

Mia bounced Cora on her shoulder. The kid was working up to a major screaming fit. "I'll be ready."

Her smile reached all the way down to his toes.

"Good. I'll look forward to it."

In his truck, away from the temptation that was Mia, he wondered if he had it in him to watch a woman walk away from him a second time. Tara's defection had hurt his pride, but whenever it came time for Mia to leave, he'd be in danger of getting down on the floor to beg.

His damaged business served as a welcome distraction even now. Fortunately, the Silver Dollar was in good shape. Water had seeped in around one of the ground-floor doors, but since repairs hadn't begun, it was no big deal.

He grabbed a cup of coffee from a shop near his business and took a moment to call Zoe, who was delighted to be tapped as a babysitter. When he finished his drink, he walked down one of the side streets, gazing in each window. Silver Glen boasted numerous unique shops.

He paused in front of an antique store. There in the window was a collection of silver charms. One caught his eye. A book. The tiny piece of silver seemed to encapsulate the very thing that had brought Mia into his life in the beginning. On a whim, he went inside and bought the charm and a bracelet to match.

On the way home, his excitement mounted. Dinner with a beautiful woman. The possibility of sharing her bed later tonight. It didn't get much better than that.

When he entered the house, it was strangely quiet. He grabbed a water bottle out of the fridge and only then spotted the note on the kitchen table.

Dylan—

Cora and I are napping. Don't let us sleep past four-thirty. I'll need time to get ready.

Mia

He tucked the note in his shirt pocket, grinning. Neither he nor Mia had gotten much sleep last night. To keep himself from climbing into bed *with* her, he decided that now was as good a time as any to look over the tax stuff she wanted him to see.

His office was neat as a pin…far tidier than he ever managed to keep it. Gertie was banned from this room. The housekeeper rearranged his stacks and made it impossible for him to find things.

The laptop he'd given Mia was on the desk where she left it…and it was turned on. She must have gotten up abruptly to tend to Cora. He used the touch pad to wake things up and saw immediately that Mia's email was on the screen.

His first impulse was to click out of it. He wasn't the kind of man who snooped in other people's stuff. But even with only a brief glance, one word jumped off the screen. *Interview.* His gut tightened as he sat down to read the rest, unable to help himself.

The sender had merely replied to a message from Mia, so Dylan was able to scroll down and see what she had written. It sounded like she had sent more of these letters, all indicating her availability and asking about possible job openings.

Even as his stomach tightened, he told himself it made perfect sense. Mia hadn't kept any secrets from him. Of course she had been looking for future employment. Still, the email felt like a betrayal. An illogical response on his part, but true.

The original email had an attachment. He clicked on the word *résumé* and hit Print. Pages began spitting out of his printer. Gathering them up, he sat down in a chair and started to read...slowly, as always.

Any dreams he had begun to weave about keeping Mia in Silver Glen disintegrated into something that resembled the ashes of a hot fire. Mia had earned not one, but *two* PhDs from prestigious universities. Her work history was impressive, but what he found the most daunting were her research and writing credits.

Over two pages of the résumé were devoted to lists of Mia's articles published in academic journals, as well as papers she had presented at scientific conferences all over the U.S. and around the world.

He had fooled himself into thinking of Mia as a simple, down-to-earth mother of a new baby. Helping Mia and Cora had made him feel like a man. He liked having them look to him for support.

But the truth was far less cozy. He'd been right in the first place. Mia didn't belong in Silver Glen. And she would never belong to him. Even if she wanted him physically.

Calmly, he fed the pages into a shredder. Then he went to the living room and sat down to wait.

* * *

Mia had only napped forty-five minutes, but she awoke feeling refreshed and energetic. A peep in at Cora told her the baby still slept. If Mia was lucky, she might have time to pick out an outfit before her daughter demanded attention.

The impulse to dance around the room made her sheepish. Yes, she was going to have dinner with her lover. And yes, he wanted to talk to her…in private. But that could mean anything.

Her nap had left her mouth feeling cottony, so she headed to the kitchen for a glass of the iced tea Gertie kept on hand round the clock. When she was halfway across the living room, she stopped short, her hand to her chest. "Dylan. You startled me. I didn't expect you back so soon. Is everything at the Silver Dollar okay?"

"Everything at the saloon is fine. No change." He sat sprawled in an armchair, a beer in his right hand and his legs stretched out in front of him. He wasn't smiling. And he didn't look the least bit amorous.

Gradually, a feeling of alarm squashed Mia's euphoria. "What happened, then? You look…" She trailed off, unable to decide what was wrong with the picture.

The fingers of his left hand drummed on the arm of the chair. That slight movement was the only visible sign that he was upset. "I changed my mind about dinner," he said.

She sank into a seat opposite him, her heart at her feet. "I see."

"I doubt you do." Fatigue and bitterness nuanced his words.

"Then why don't you explain?"

He reached into the pocket of his pants and pulled out a folded check. Tossing it on the coffee table beside a small white box, he grimaced. "I hired you in good faith. So I've written that for six months' pay. It should be enough to help you and Cora make a new start in Raleigh. The other thing is a little gift that reminded me of you."

When she bit down hard on her lower lip, she tasted the rusty tang of blood. "I don't understand. I thought you wanted me here. I thought you wanted *me*."

His gaze was bleak. "What I want doesn't matter. You have a job offer. I saw the email. When I went to look at the tax forms." He stopped. She saw the muscles in his throat work. "I need you to leave, Mia. You don't belong here. Go home. Go back to the life you were meant for. Take what you need in the short-term and when you have an address, let me know and I'll ship the rest."

She rose to her feet, frantic. "I don't want to leave. I don't know what's happened, but please don't do this."

For a moment, she thought her plea had gotten through to him. His left hand curled into a fist, and his right hand gripped the beer bottle white-knuckled.

Long seconds ticked by.

Then, with every ounce of expression wiped from his face, he stood up, his gaze landing anywhere but on her. "I'm sleeping up at the hotel tonight. I'd like you to be gone by noon tomorrow. If you need Gertie's help in packing, her number's in the kitchen. Goodbye, Mia."

The six weeks that followed were some of the worst of Mia's life, harder even than when she had welcomed a newborn into her home. The drive back to Raleigh was a blur she barely remembered. Fortunately, Cora had been a doll, napping peacefully for most of the trip.

After one night in a chain motel, Mia hit rock-bottom. She didn't have the luxury of tearing Dylan's check into tiny pieces. If it had been only her, she would have slept in her car before she would have accepted his money. But she had Cora to think of, Cora to protect. Sometimes a parent had to make hard choices.

Once Mia took Dylan's check to the bank, the train was set in motion. With what was left in her checking and savings accounts, and with the generous termination settlement Dylan had given her, there was enough to put down deposits on a nice apartment.

For the moment, Cora slept on the carpet beside her mother. Mia purchased a sleeping bag for herself. Eventually she would get some things out of storage, but for now she was hiding out. Since she had already talked to her friends and told them she was staying in Silver Glen for a while, how could she explain her unexpected return?

From her phone, she emailed the department head who had offered an interview and told him a family situation had put her plans on hold. After that, all she did was play with her daughter and weep. The crying jags ended after the first week. It wasn't good for the baby to see her mother so unhappy. Mia decided that by living only in the present, she could pretend that everything was normal.

She lost weight. Only the prospect of her milk drying up induced her to eat at all. Nursing Cora was a lifeline. It kept her sane. Made her feel whole. She had to take in enough calories to keep feeding her daughter.

Sometimes, if it wasn't too hot, they went for a walk in the park. She had brought Cora's stroller with her from Dylan's house. Amongst other families pushing infants along the paths, she could almost pretend that she was going to be okay.

But at night, when Cora slept, dreams of Dylan kept Mia awake. Ironically, now that she would not have minded Cora's company in the middle of the night, the baby slept from eight in the evening until eight the next morning.

At the end of the second week, Dylan texted her and asked where to send her things. In a panic, she went to the phone store and had her number changed. Even that minimal contact with the man in Silver Glen, the man she loved who had broken her heart, threatened her fragile composure.

Her entire world had imploded, and she didn't know what to do. On the basis of one stupid email, Dylan had decided that Mia needed to go back to her career. But that wasn't his decision to make. Yes, she loved her work, and yes, it was important. But did that trump love? Why couldn't Dylan fight for her? Why couldn't he let her make her own decisions?

In truth, though, she couldn't see a clear answer. Short of Dylan moving to Raleigh—and that seemed wrong on many levels—she didn't see a solution. If Dylan's feelings for her had been stronger, she might have decided to put her career on hold. But even that seemed like a poor choice.

By the time August rolled toward a steamy end, heading for the Labor Day weekend and the official end of summer, Mia had managed to reach deep inside herself and draw on reserves of strength she hadn't known existed. For her child's sake, she had to pick up the pieces of her life.

Cora was growing rapidly and needed new clothes. One blistering afternoon after naptime, Mia loaded the baby into the car and found a mall, one in a part of town she had never frequented. She still couldn't bear the thought of running into anyone she knew.

By the time she wrestled the stroller out of the trunk, lifted Cora out of her car seat, and trudged across the hot pavement into the mall, she felt dizzy and sick. Instead of heading to a department store, she made her way to the food court. All she could think about was buying a large, icy-cold soda.

As she rummaged in her purse for her billfold, she staggered, putting out her hand and grabbing for support. The young man behind the counter stared. "You okay, ma'am?"

Mia licked her lips, trying to breathe. Yellow spots danced in front of her eyes. "Yes," she whispered. "No problem." And then her world went black....

Seventeen

Dylan was frantic. When Mia didn't respond to his text, he hired a private-detective agency to find her...to make sure she and the baby were okay. But everywhere they looked they hit a dead end. It was as if Mia had disappeared from the face of the earth.

She cashed his check. That knowledge gave him a tiny bit of comfort. At least he didn't have to worry that Mia and Cora were destitute. But when he tried to have her phone calls traced, he knew she had deliberately changed her number.

In the intervening weeks, as he missed Mia and Cora with a raw pain that kept him awake at night, he realized he had given up without a fight. And that was not like him. He had been wrong to make them leave. He began to think of solutions, and if none of those panned out, he was ready to pack up and move to Raleigh.

Desperation drove him to extreme measures. Though it was immoral if not downright illegal, he found a tech guru who was willing to hack into the computer Mia had used in Dylan's office. The man tapped into her email account, but there was only one outgoing email. A note informing the sender that she would not be interviewing for a job, the job Dylan had seen earlier.

If Mia wasn't trying to find a job, then what in the hell was she doing? He even checked hospitals throughout the

Raleigh/Durham area in case either Mia or Cora was ill or injured.

The computer geek had showed him how to access the email himself. Every morning and every evening, Dylan sat with the laptop, praying for something, anything. But apparently, Mia was not using her email at all.

His break came in an unexpected way. One morning, an email from her bank popped up with the heading "address change." Without compunction, he opened it, jotted down the information and ran to his bedroom to pack a bag. Six hours later, he parked in front of a nondescript block of apartments.

With his heart pounding and his chest tight, he searched for the numbers that identified the units. There it was.

When Mia opened the door, her face went pale with shock. "What are you doing here?" Animosity crackled in every syllable.

"I came to apologize," he said. "May I come in?"

In case she decided to be obstructive, he didn't wait for an answer, but instead, eased his way past her into the tiny efficiency apartment. He stopped short. Now it was his turn to be shocked. The space was virtually empty. A camp chair sat in the living room in front of him. A portable crib and a sleeping bag occupied the central section of the carpeted floor. There were no other items of furniture. No television, no sofa, no bed.

Dylan's net worth amounted to over three million dollars. Yet, the woman he loved was sleeping on the floor every night. Guilt for what he had done to her sickened him. Fury raged in his chest for his own stupidity. He had to convince Mia that he was sorry. That he was wrong to send her away. That he loved her too much to let her go. He had a feeling his negotiation skills were going to be tested to the limit.

Projecting a calm he didn't feel, he walked past Mia's

single chair and lowered himself to the floor, his back against a wall. "We need to talk."

She glared at him. "The last time you said that it was a prelude to kicking me out of your house."

Swallowing hard, he took the hit without trying to justify his actions. "Please, Mia. Let me say what I came to say." She looked ill, and that worried him more than anything.

"If that's what it takes to get rid of you, fine." Instead of taking the chair, she copied his pose, leaning against the adjacent wall.

Cora was asleep, so he kept his voice low. "I'm sorry for being an arrogant, insensitive jerk. It was presumptuous of me to think I knew what was best for you, for your life, for Cora."

"And what brought about this monumental change of heart?" Now he could see the grief in her gaze. Grief that could and should be laid firmly at his door.

"You left." He said it bluntly, willing her to understand.

"And?"

"And I realized how much I loved you. Well," he said, backtracking, "I was pretty sure about that *before* you left. But my empty house sealed the deal. I also realized that I had tried to play God with your future. As if you were not smart enough to choose your own path. And when you think about it, that makes me look pretty stupid."

"You're not stupid." Her response was automatic.

She'd said those same three words to him more than a decade ago and again when she returned to Silver Glen. The trouble was, he hadn't been able to hear them.

"Let's just say that I'm willing to learn from my mistakes."

"Okay. You're forgiven. Please leave."

"Not so fast," he said, stung by her rejection, though he undoubtedly deserved it. "I want a do-over."

"I don't know what that means."

As he studied her face, he was struck by the way her cheekbones stood out and by the dark smudges beneath her eyes. "You look terrible," he blurted out.

"Is that your idea of a do-over?"

For the first time he saw a glimmer of amusement on her face. "Sorry," he muttered. "I've been worried as hell about you."

"I'm not your responsibility."

They seemed to be going in circles. "Mia." He stopped, searched his heart, and did the best he could. He'd made a lot of mistakes in his life, but none he wanted to fix more than this one. "I didn't give you a choice before. I didn't ask what *you* wanted. That's why I'm here now. I need to know what *you* want. What will make *you* happy." He gave the tiny apartment a disparaging glance. "Surely not this place."

"I've moved on, Dylan. I'm making a new start. I'm not the same woman you booted out of your life eight weeks ago."

"Have you been sick?" He had to know.

She shrugged. "In a manner of speaking. When I left Silver Glen, I had a severe relapse into postpartum depression. But don't worry," she said quickly. "I'm under a doctor's care, and I'm going to be fine. I have three job interviews in the next two weeks. Cora and I are back on our feet."

"But are you happy?"

It hadn't escaped his notice that he'd told her he loved her and she never even acknowledged his declaration.

She looked down at her lap where her hands twisted and clenched. "I'm content. I think happiness is a bit of a myth. I'm focusing on Cora and her well-being. That's what matters to me now."

"Happiness is *not* a myth. It's real. And I'll ask you

again. What do *you* want, Mia? If I hadn't been such a jackass, what would have made you happy in Silver Glen?" She had never said she loved him, but she had hinted at it. Why wouldn't she express that emotion now? Had he hurt her too badly for her to ever trust him again?

"Please go, Dylan." Her face was the color of skim milk.

He scooted across the distance that separated them and sat beside her, hip to hip. "You're wearing the bracelet I gave you." He toyed with the book charm, his fingertips brushing the back of her hand.

"It entertains the baby."

He ignored her ridiculous explanation. "I want to marry you, Mia."

He felt her body jerk, but she didn't say a word. So he forged ahead doggedly. "I may as well spell it out, so you know where I stand. But keep in mind that all of this is subject to your approval…to *your* wants and needs."

Needing badly to connect with her, he took her hand in his, clasping her fingers and resting their linked hands on his thigh. She didn't pull away. So maybe there was still hope. "My family has the means to build a research facility in Silver Glen. We could bring in top-notch scientists from all over the world. You could run the whole thing, or we could outfit a lab just for you and the projects that are important to you. I can hire a manager for the Silver Dollar so I'll be free to keep Cora while you work. I'd like to adopt her if it's okay with you." He ran out of steam, his heart sinking to the soles of his feet. Mia had all the animation of a block of wood, not exactly the kind of response a man looks for when he proposes.

Finally, when he began to feel foolish and depressed all at the same time, Mia stood up to pace. She paused on the far side of the room. "I appreciate your apology and your proposal…or all of your proposals," she said quietly. "But I have to say no."

Was it possible for a man to feel his heart shatter?

Swallowing the lump of regret and grief in his throat, he stood as well. "Why, Mia? Why do you have to say no?" In his bed and in his arms, he could have sworn that she felt something for him.

She rubbed her temples with her fingertips, her posture defeated. "I'm pregnant, Dylan."

Mia's emotions were all over the map. When all the color leached from Dylan's face, he slid down the wall, his butt thumping the ground. "How? Is it another man?"

Rolling her eyes, she shook her head. "Now you *are* being stupid. Of course not. Do you remember that night when we made love half-asleep? Actually, it was toward morning. Neither of us thought to use protection."

She saw the moment when he remembered. Some expression crossed his face, one she couldn't discern. "I don't know what to say." His words were raspy as if he could barely speak.

"It isn't your fault. We were both in that bed. And you've made it abundantly clear that you don't intend to father any children. You'll have access, of course, if you want it."

"If I want it?" He parroted the words, clearly in shock.

"I know this is a lot to absorb, but your life won't change. You don't have to worry about anything. I can handle this."

He shook his head as if trying to dismiss the remnants of a bad dream. When he rose to his feet a second time, alarm skittered down her spine. His black scowl promised retribution. "Are you insane? Of course I want my child!"

She refused to be frightened by his bluster. They had to clear this up once and for all. "But what if your son or daughter takes after you? What if your child has dyslexia?

Or bad eyesight? Or a heart murmur? Or isn't coordinated? What if he or she does poorly in school?"

He put his hand over her mouth and drew her close. "You've made your point, Mia." His lopsided smile broadened with dawning wonder. "My God, a baby." He touched her flat belly with reverence. "We're going to be parents. Cora will have a sibling." He kissed her hard. A possessive mating of teeth and tongues and ragged breath that took the starch out of her knees.

Mia's eyes stung with tears when they separated, her throat tight. "I love you, Dylan, very much. But I have to be sure where you stand. You can't kick us to the curb every time I get an award or receive recognition for my work. I have to know that our relationship is one of equals."

He understood what she was saying. And he wasn't foolish enough to think everything would be easy. But none of that was critical in the end. "I'm so proud of you, Mia. I'll always be proud of you. But what matters to me now is far more important than your brain. I see the love in your heart. For Cora. For me. I want to be the man who makes *you* proud. Your friend. Your lover. Cora's father. I love you, Mia. For always."

She searched his face with a gaze full of hesitant wonder. "You really mean it, don't you? You understand."

"It's taken me a while," he said quietly. "But yes. I do."

She flung herself against him, her arms tightening around his neck in a stranglehold. "I adore you, Dylan Kavanagh."

Stroking her hair, he propped his chin on top of her head. "Pretty soon, word's going to get out about us and it will be pretty clear that *I'm* the smart one for snapping you up."

"You're such a flatterer. But I like it."

He pulled back and took her hands in his. "We'll get

married this weekend," he said. "My family knows everyone in Silver Glen. We can do it at the hotel, or a church if
you'd prefer. Zoe can help you find a dress…."

Mia put a hand over *his* mouth. "This isn't going to be
easy for you, is it? Letting me make decisions?"

He nipped her fingers with his teeth. "We'll probably
argue a lot. And have wild, incredible makeup sex. I love
you, Mia, more than you'll ever understand, even with
that genius brain of yours."

He went still as she cupped his cheeks in her hands
and searched his eyes for the truth. What she saw must
have reassured her, because when she spoke, the words
were confident and strong. "I want to spend time with our
children before they start school. It's important to me. But
with what you're suggesting about the lab, I can work from
home, or utilize a flex schedule."

Dylan sobered. "*Our* children." The reality was sinking in at last. He and Mia had built a family. The rush of
exhilaration weakened his knees. "Then you will have
your wish. And in that case…" He stepped back enough
to take her hands.

"Yes?"

He paused, swallowing hard. "I'd like to go back to
school and finish a degree. With your help."

Mia hadn't known she could love him any more. "Will
you believe me when I say it doesn't matter to me? I love
you, Dylan Kavanagh. And I always will."

"Not for you," he said quietly, his eyes alight with happiness. "For me. For Cora. And for this one." He placed
both of his hands on her stomach. "I have a feeling I'm
going to have more than one genius on my hands, and I
need to be able to keep up."

She laid her head against his chest, feeling the wonderfully steady beat of his heart. "You're going to be a wonderful father."

"And lover," he reminded helpfully.

"That, too."

Dylan glanced around the small room that had been her hideout for long, miserable weeks. "I think we're done here, Mia, my love. Let's take Cora and go home. You're both mine now. For keeps."

* * * * *

If you liked Dylan's story,
pick up his brother Liam's tale,
both part of the **KAVANAGHS OF SILVER GLEN**
from USA TODAY bestselling author Janice Maynard!

A NOT-SO-INNOCENT SEDUCTION

Available now from Harlequin Desire!

If you liked this Billionaires & Babies novel,
watch for the next book in this #1 bestselling
Desire series,
THE SHEIKH'S SON
by Kristi Gold,
available July 2014.

#2311 HER PREGNANCY SECRET
by Ann Major
Though he believes Bree is a gold digger, Michael nonetheless agrees to care for his brother's pregnant widow. But as duty turns to passion, what will he do when he discovers the shocking truth about her pregnancy?

#2312 LURED BY THE RICH RANCHER
Dynasties: The Lassiters • by Kathie DeNosky
Hired to restore the Lassiters' public image, Fee finds the perfect man in Chance Lassiter—for her campaign that is! Opposites attract when this city girl experiences firsthand the charms of the country—and a handsome cowboy.

#2313 THE SHEIKH'S SON
Billionaires and Babies • by Kristi Gold
Faced with raising the infant son he didn't know existed, Sheikh Mehdi marries for convenience. But the desirable Piper McAdams sees the man behind the devil-may-care sheikh, and for the first time, love may be within his grasp.

#2314 A TASTE OF TEMPTATION
Las Vegas Nights • by Cat Schield
Globe-trotting celebrity chef Ashton Croft meets his match in hotel executive Harper. But when a shocking family secret turns her life upside down, Ashton must decide if he wants to be her rock or a rolling stone.

#2315 MATCHED TO A BILLIONAIRE
Happily Ever After, Inc. • by Kat Cantrell
Needing a wife in name only, Leo Reynolds hires a matchmaker to find him the perfect partner—the sophisticated Daniella. But soon Leo wants to renegotiate the terms of their contract—in the bedroom!

#2316 WHEN OPPOSITES ATTRACT...
The Barrington Trilogy • by Jules Bennett
Working on location brings up painful memories as Hollywood hotshot Grant Carter is thrust into an equestrian world—jockey Tessa Barrington's world. But the innocent Tessa proves a temptation he'll risk everything for, even facing his traumatic past.

———————

HDCNM0614

REQUEST YOUR FREE BOOKS!
2 FREE NOVELS PLUS 2 FREE GIFTS!

HARLEQUIN®

Desire

ALWAYS POWERFUL, PASSIONATE AND PROVOCATIVE

YES! Please send me 2 FREE Harlequin Desire® novels and my 2 FREE gifts (gifts are worth about $10). After receiving them, if I don't wish to receive any more books, I can return the shipping statement marked "cancel." If I don't cancel, I will receive 6 brand-new novels every month and be billed just $4.55 per book in the U.S. or $4.99 per book in Canada. That's a savings of at least 13% off the cover price! It's quite a bargain! Shipping and handling is just 50¢ per book in the U.S. and 75¢ per book in Canada.* I understand that accepting the 2 free books and gifts places me under no obligation to buy anything. I can always return a shipment and cancel at any time. Even if I never buy another book, the two free books and gifts are mine to keep forever.

225/326 HDN F4ZC

Name _____ (PLEASE PRINT) _____

Address _____ Apt. #

City _____ State/Prov. _____ Zip/Postal Code

Signature (if under 18, a parent or guardian must sign)

Mail to the Harlequin® Reader Service:
IN U.S.A.: P.O. Box 1867, Buffalo, NY 14240-1867
IN CANADA: P.O. Box 609, Fort Erie, Ontario L2A 5X3

Want to try two free books from another line?
Call 1-800-873-8635 or visit www.ReaderService.com.

* Terms and prices subject to change without notice. Prices do not include applicable taxes. Sales tax applicable in N.Y. Canadian residents will be charged applicable taxes. Offer not valid in Quebec. This offer is limited to one order per household. Not valid for current subscribers to Harlequin Desire books. All orders subject to credit approval. Credit or debit balances in a customer's account(s) may be offset by any other outstanding balance owed by or to the customer. Please allow 4 to 6 weeks for delivery. Offer available while quantities last.

Your Privacy—The Harlequin® Reader Service is committed to protecting your privacy. Our Privacy Policy is available online at www.ReaderService.com or upon request from the Harlequin Reader Service.

We make a portion of our mailing list available to reputable third parties that offer products we believe may interest you. If you prefer that we not exchange your name with third parties, or if you wish to clarify or modify your communication preferences, please visit us at www.ReaderService.com/consumerschoice or write to us at Harlequin Reader Service Preference Service, P.O. Box 9062, Buffalo, NY 14269. Include your complete name and address.

HD13R

Turn the page for a sneak peek at USA TODAY
bestselling author **Kathie DeNosky's**

LURED BY THE RICH RANCHER, the fourth novel in
Harlequin Desire's **DYNASTIES: THE LASSITERS** *series.*

It's city vs. country when Chance Lassiter meets
PR exec Felicity Sinclair....

"**W**ould you like to dance, Ms. Sinclair?"

She glanced at her uncomfortable-looking high heels.
"I...hadn't thought I would be dancing."

Laughing, Chance Lassiter bent down to whisper close
to her ear. "I'm from the school of stand in one place and
sway."

Her delightful laughter caused a warm feeling to spread
throughout his chest. "I think that's about all I'll be able to
do in these shoes anyway."

When she placed her soft hand in his and stood up to walk
out onto the dance floor with him, an electric current shot
straight up his arm. He wrapped his arms loosely around her
and smiled down at her upturned face.

"Chance, there's something I'd like to discuss with you,"
she said as they swayed back and forth.

"I'm all ears," he said, grinning.

"I'd like your help with my public relations campaign to
improve the Lassiters' image."

"Sure. I'll do whatever I can to help you out," he said,
drawing her a little closer. "What did you have in mind?"

"You're going to be the family spokesman for the PR campaign that I'm planning," she said, beaming.

Marveling at how beautiful she was, it took a moment for her words to register with him. He stopped swaying and stared down at her in disbelief. "You want me to do what?"

"I'm going to have you appear in all future advertising for Lassiter Media," she said, sounding extremely excited. "You'll be in the national television commercials, as well as…"

Chance silently ran through every cuss word he'd ever heard. He might be a Lassiter, but he wasn't as refined as the rest of the family. Instead of riding a desk in some corporate office, he was on the back of a horse every day herding cattle under the wide Wyoming sky. That was the way he liked it and the way he intended for things to stay. There was no way in hell he was going to be the family spokesman. And the sooner he could find a way to get that across to her, the better.

Don't miss
LURED BY THE RICH RANCHER
by Kathie DeNosky.

Available July 2014,
wherever Harlequin® Desire books are sold.